LJ BURKHART

Fire & Ink

A Fire Novel

First edition

This book was professionally typeset on Reedsy.
Find out more at reedsy.com

Contents

Chapter 1

Savannah

I wiped my brow as I looked at the clock. Three hours in. One more hour and I could call it a day. This was my last tattoo today, and all I could think about was getting a drink. My eyes reluctantly made their way back to my client's thigh. It was a pretty sick-looking tiger, if I did say so myself. I had been working on this design for a couple weeks now. The cat's body curved up the side of her leg like the fierce predator he was. His tail circled around the back of her knee and ended just below it at the top of her shin. His body was going to be shaded beautifully with reds, oranges, black, and white. I was currently finishing with the oranges and was about to move on to the reds.

"How are you doing, Lauren? Ready for a little break before I start in on the red?" I asked.

"Yeah, I think my skin would be grateful, and I could really use a cigarette," she replied.

"Yeah, I could use one too. Why don't you go out front and I'll meet you in just a minute?" I shouldn't be smoking, considering I was trying to cut back and quit eventually, but it had been a long day.

I started to the back of the shop where the restrooms were and locked

1

the door behind me. I hated this bathroom. So cold and dingy. The lighting was dim and the tiles and the walls were both a cool gray. Its only redeeming quality was the artwork. Pictures of Marilyn Monroe over the steaming grate and what Audrey Hepburn would look like all tatted up hung on the walls. I finished up quickly and washed my hands before going to find my purse, where my smokes were. Damn. Only one left. I grabbed it and my lighter and made my way out front.

Lauren was already halfway through her cigarette when I joined her. It was eight o'clock and I was starving. I hadn't had time to eat before she got here, and I thought I would be okay for a few hours. I always forgot how hungry I get while working.

"Man, I'm hungry," Lauren said to me just as I was thinking it. "What are you doing after this? Wanna go grab a drink and some food when we're finished?" she asked me.

"Sure, I would love to! I'll have to clean up though. Are you willing to wait?"

"Yeah, absolutely. I'm in no rush. It's not like I have anything else to do."

She laughed. Lauren had just moved here from Michigan about a month or two ago. She told me earlier that she had grown up in "the pinky" and had a group of high school friends that she still talked to and missed pretty fiercely, but she hadn't had a chance to make any here yet.

"Yeah, I know how that goes. I'm so busy lately I don't have time to do anything but work, eat, and sleep," I said as we headed back inside. "Let me just wash my hands and we can finish up the last of that wicked tiger." I winked as I went to the sink.

I dried my hands and returned to my room to find Lauren already back on the table. I turned the music up, put my gloves on, and went to work. "The Sharpest Lives" by My Chemical Romance was on—my own playlist of hard rock, metal, and alternative. I was the last person at work tonight and that meant I could put on whatever I damn well pleased.

"Wow, I really love this playlist. Is this Pandora?"

"No, actually. Just on my iTunes. I call this my gym playlist 'cause it really gets me moving. I'm the newest here so I don't usually get first dibs on the music, but no one else is here tonight so I have free rein," I said to her as I dabbed the needle into the red ink.

"Yeah, I have one of those too. Sometimes I just get into the mood to rock the fuck out. I don't think my boyfriend gets it. He listens mostly to underground hip-hop."

"Oh really? I listen to some of that. My friend got me into A Tribe Called Quest when I was younger. I can even rap a little for you, if you're ever curious," I said with a chuckle.

We continued chatting about music and her boyfriend as I finished up her tattoo.

"Okay, Lauren, let me just wipe you down and then I'll let you look at it before I wrap it up." I sprayed some green soap solution on a paper towel and wiped off all the extra ink and blood. Man, I loved this piece. Then again, I loved anything related to felines and was always really stoked when someone asked for them. "All right, you can go take a look in the mirror and see what you think." I watched her walk across the room as I waited for her reaction. I was always a bit apprehensive for this part. There was always a very small voice in my head, *his* voice, that said that nothing I ever did would ever be good enough. It was also slightly nerve-racking to hear the person who would have this on their body forever critique your work.

"Oh, I love it! Thank you so much. It looks even better than I imagined!" Lauren exclaimed and I sighed with relief. Hers was the reaction I got most of the time from people, and it always made up for the anxiety I felt. She stood there twisting her leg around so she could see it all.

"Oh good. I'm so glad you love it. I had a lot of fun designing this one so thanks for coming to me with it! Let me just bandage you up and then we can head out for that drink. Where do you wanna go?" I asked as I wiped her down once more.

"I was hearing that The Matador was pretty cool. That's not too far, is it?" she asked while I applied Aquaphor and Saran Wrap around her leg.

"No, it's only a few blocks down actually. I've been there before and I really liked it. Nice choice."

We headed up front and I slid behind the counter to figure out how much I was going to charge her. I rattled off the price as she started digging around in her wallet for cash. She counted out the amount and added in a generous tip.

"Thanks so much, lady. I'm really glad Veronica gave you my information," I said. "Why don't you head to the restaurant and save us a spot? I need to clean up real quick and then I'll meet you over there."

"Me too! This is definitely the best work I've had done. It looks like you're stuck with me as your client," she said and laughed. "But yes, I will go grab us a seat. Take as long as you need cleaning up and I'll see you soon!"

Lauren walked out the door and I followed to lock it behind her. I turned the music up to rock out while I tidied. This was probably my least favorite part of the job. There was always so much to clean. I stopped my mental bitching and got to work. The sooner I left, the sooner I could get wasted. I put my ass into gear and scrubbed everything down, paying special attention to my table and all of my instruments. Forty-five minutes later, I had my station cleaned, the drawer counted, and the lobby tidied up. I turned the stereo and the lights off and headed out the back door. I made sure it was locked behind me and unlocked my little silver car. God, I loved it. It fit my personality perfectly. A 2010 VW Jetta. Manual transmission and a sunroof that I opened up when I was feeling sassy (which was most of the time) and wanted to feel the air all around me. I hooked up my iPhone and cranked my music up as I turned out of the back lot. A few minutes later I pulled up to the restaurant on 32nd and Lowell. I got out of my car after finding a parking spot about a block away.

I opened the door to the bar and was immediately struck by a cacophony of sounds. I spotted Lauren sitting at a table and made my way over to her. She already had an extra dirty martini in front of her and waved as soon as she saw me. I plopped down in the seat next to her.

"Hey, bitch," I said to her. "How's that martini treating you? It looks delicious."

"You call your friends 'bitch' too? I do that all the time!" she laughed. "And this is just what I needed. This is already my second one."

"Looks like I have some catching up to do." As if on cue, the waitress came up and asked what I wanted to drink. "I think I'll have what she's having," I told her as I proceeded to get out my ID.

"Coming right up, hun," she said as she walked away.

"Did they drop us off any menus? I'm starving. I would kill for a burrito."

"Yes, they're right here. Sorry, I was hoarding them."

She handed over a menu and I looked it over as the waitress brought my martini. I took a nice long drink of it and ate an olive as soon as she dropped it off. Oh my God, everything looked so good. I love burritos, so of course that was on my list of options. I finally settled on the tacos al carbon. I absolutely loved Mexican food; I often felt I was a Mexican chica trapped in a white girl's body. I took Spanish in high school but I got nervous speaking it, so I lost a lot of it. The waitress came back and took our orders, and I asked for another martini. I was only halfway through mine but figured I would order it while she was here.

"So, how are you liking Colorado so far?" I asked Lauren when the server walked away.

"I love it here! Much different from Michigan, but not in a bad way. Lots more to do, more people, not to mention that I can smoke weed legally now," she said and we laughed. "I'm still looking for a job though. My boyfriend, Ryan, had to move out here for work, and I love him too much not to be with him, so here I am! But it was pretty short notice, so it's been hectic getting everything together and sorted out."

"Oh you're such a good girlfriend!" I teased her. "That sucks that you haven't found a place to work yet. You said you were a hair stylist before you moved here, right?"

"Yeah. I've been doing hair for about seven years now. I took classes while I was still in high school, which was convenient. As soon as I graduated, I was able to start working and move out of my parents' place. I don't know if I want to keep cutting hair though. I'm kinda over it. But I don't know what else I would do. Maybe I should just get a boring desk job somewhere. I feel like that would definitely be easier than dealing with smug bitches whining about how their hair is not the *exact* shade of blonde they wanted. I don't miss that at all."

I laughed. I knew exactly how that went. "At least you don't have to deal with sorority girls coming in and wanting their house name tattooed on all ten of them, thinking that's the most original idea ever. God, I hate that shit. Makes me very glad I never went to college."

"Oh, me too. I don't think I would have been able to go one day without beating a bitch down," she said and we both laughed.

I felt a breeze as the door opened and in walked one of the most gorgeous men I had ever seen. He definitely had major potential to break some hearts. He had dark brown hair that was pulled back into a bun, a decent beard, and dark emerald-green eyes. He was wearing dark blue jeans and an Alkaline Trio T-shirt. His right arm was full of tattoos in a sleeve all the way to his wrist with one curved around his thumb. He walked up to the bar, ordered a drink, and glanced my way.

6

I quickly averted my eyes so he wouldn't notice my ogling.

I looked around hoping that our food wouldn't be too much longer. Just as I had the thought, I saw it coming down the aisle toward us. Shit, it smelled so good. I took the last drink of my first martini so it would be out of the way of our food. As soon as our server set it down, I dug in. It was very unladylike, but I didn't care. It tasted so damn good. I looked at Lauren and she was doing the exact same thing with her fajitas.

Ten minutes and no conversation later, our plates were cleared and we were back to our martinis. We were just joking about how we would need to hit the gym first thing tomorrow, when I looked up to see a man strutting toward the table. He was eyeing me up and down with the stupidest-looking grin on his face. I guessed he thought that it was charming, but it just came off as creepy. He looked like a thirty-five-year-old frat boy. He was starting to lose his hair, and he had on a polo shirt and khakis. And don't you know it, his collar was popped. He stumbled a little upon reaching our table. Definitely drunk then. Great.

"Hey, sexy lady," he said, leaning in closer to me. Gross. His breath reeked of Jim Beam and stale cigarettes. "How would you like to come home with me tonight? I bet you look even hotter out of your clothes."

"No, thanks," I said, turning back to Lauren, hoping he would get the message and leave. Unfortunately, it didn't seem to work.

"Let me at least buy you a drink. You look thirsty. You know you want to," he said as he winked at me and ran his clammy, pudgy hand down my arm. If I had any doubt before that he was as slimy as he looked, I didn't now.

"I said no, asshole."

"Oh, come on, sweet cheeks. I have quite a bit of money. That's my Camaro out front. We could go for a ride."

"Oh, now I want to," I said sarcastically. "Seriously, dude, I have a rule not to fuck guys with polo shirts or popped collars, so I think you

7

are shit out of luck." Lauren almost choked on her drink trying not to laugh.

"Hey, you bitch," he snarled as he grabbed me by my hair and pulled me close to him. "You better shut your mouth before I shut it for you." Then just as he was about to crush his mouth to mine, he was yanked off of me.

"I believe the lady said to get lost." It took me a second to realize that the delicious man from earlier was now standing over the old frat boy. "Now why don't you scurry off to your frat house before I have to teach you a lesson on how to treat women?" Creeper looked as if he was about to piss his pants and quickly got up to leave. Turning to face me, the future star of my fantasies asked, "Are you okay? He didn't hurt you, did he?"

I lost all brain power when he looked into my eyes. He was even more glorious up close. My eyes zeroed in on his chest and all the defined muscles I could see through his shirt. They made their way up to his face; he had a nice strong jaw and defined cheekbones. And his eyes. Dear Lord, they were like jewels. It was a few moments before I realized that he was staring at me with concern and waiting for me to answer.

"No, I'm fine. I could've handled it, you know," I said. I had mixed feelings about him coming to my rescue. On one hand, it was incredibly sexy and very gallant of him. On the other hand, I hated when men assumed that I couldn't take care of myself. Yes, I was a woman, but I could kick some serious ass if need be, and that guy he had just taken care of was about to get a knee to the balls before he walked up. He would've been lucky to have any function down there after I was done with him.

"Well, I handled it for you so you didn't have to," he said, looking amused at how perturbed I was about him coming to save me. Asshole. I didn't need his help, and I sure as hell didn't need his adorable know-it-all smile. I just bet he had a set of perfect dimples underneath the beard. That thought just made me angrier. "I do wish that I could've seen how you would've handled it, but I'm not sorry I came to help. I was able to meet you, and now maybe I can get your name and number before I leave?" he said, smiling at me.

"Well, thank you, but I'm not interested. Now, if you don't mind, my friend and I here are having a girls' night."

"Okay, I get the message. Have a good night," he said, smirking as he walked off.

I turned to Lauren, her mouth hanging open a little.

"What are you thinking?! He was gorgeous and he just saved you from that asshole!" Lauren practically shouted at me.

"Okay, he was really yummy, but I totally could have handled that guy on my own. I definitely didn't need him to come over here and act like I'm all helpless." Like I said, I had a problem with men acting like women couldn't do anything themselves. Granted, that probably wasn't what he was doing, but I was sensitive about it. I also really didn't like how strong of a reaction he pulled from me. Good thing he didn't touch me, I probably would've been completely powerless and would've done whatever he wanted.

"Okay, lady, but you just missed out on that hot piece of ass's phone number," she said.

I rolled my eyes and finished off my martini. She was right, but at least I would have a nice visual aid when I had playtime with myself later. I had way too many dates with my B.O.B. lately, but at least now I had a nice face and ass to go with my fantasies.

I looked at my phone. It was going on eleven and I was exhausted. It had been a nine-hour day at work and a six-day work week. Luckily, I had tomorrow off, so I could sleep in and get some cleaning done around my apartment. I signaled the waitress to bring our check. After we paid, Lauren and I headed out to our cars.

"Thanks so much for everything. I love my tattoo and I'm really glad we got to go for a drink and hang out," Lauren said as we stopped next to my car.

"Me too! We should exchange numbers and hang out again. I don't have a ton of free time, but I can definitely get together on my days off."

We pulled out our phones as we rattled off our numbers for each other. I gave her a hug goodbye and got in my little car I had named "Roxy." I arrived at my apartment about ten minutes later. As soon as I walked in, I heard my tabby cat meowing from the kitchen. *Jorge must be hungry*, I thought. Then again, he was always hungry, so I guess I shouldn't be surprised. I filled up his bowl and started petting him as he munched away. I went to my bathroom to get ready for bed. As soon as I was done, I crawled into bed, turned on some music and lay down. When Jorge was done with his dinner he came up and cuddled next to me. I fell asleep to the image in my head of a handsome brown-haired, green-eyed stranger.

Chapter 2

Charlie

As I was waiting for the light to turn green on 32nd and Lowell, I looked to my right and saw a man in his midthirties stumbling out of the bar. He tried unsuccessfully to grab some chick's ass. She turned quickly and slapped him hard across the face and walked off. He didn't seem to be too upset by it, however, and continued to cross the street in front of me just as the light changed. He took his sweet ass time making his way across, tripping over his feet a couple times. By the time he was on the other side, the light had almost changed back to red. I found a parking space about a block or so down from my destination, got out, and locked my car behind me. I made a beeline for the bar, jonesing for a drink. A strong one.

I walked in the door to The Matador and started toward the bar. Fuck, it had been such a long day. We had calls coming in all day at the fire station and I was exhausted. I was also very wired, hence the reason I was here. After I ordered my usual drink, scotch on the rocks, I took a look around. Suddenly, I noticed a stunning vixen looking at me from across the room. She quickly glanced away so that I wouldn't notice her staring. Too late. She had hair that looked like fire. The top was a dark bold red that faded into an orangish blonde at the ends. It looked like she had curled it that morning. She was wearing a tight black tank top and jeans, allowing me to see her fantastic figure. Nice wide hips, generous tits, and a slim waist. Her tank top also showed off her full sleeves of tattoos running down both arms, and I wondered where else she might have tattoos. Holy shit, I was salivating just looking at her and my dick was already at half-mast.

The bartender interrupted my thoughts as he dropped off my drink. I took a big swallow of my scotch, trying to distract myself from her. It was about ten or so and I had to work in the morning, so I wasn't planning on staying long. I turned back to the bar and sat down. There was a guy next to me who looked like he was flying solo tonight too.

"Hey, man," I said, "my name's Charlie. You on your own tonight?"

"Oh, hey. I'm Roger," he replied. "And, yeah, I am. I actually just got dumped."

"Oh, dude, that blows. I'm sorry. How about I buy you a shot and we can drink our troubles away?"

"Yeah, sure."

I signaled the bartender and ordered us two shots of Jack Daniels. He brought them over a minute later. I lifted my shot glass.

"Here's to life fucking us in the ass."

Roger chuckled and clinked his glass to mine. We chatted for the next fifteen minutes or so. He told me all about his situation and about the girl who dumped him. I just finished off my scotch when I heard shouting on the other side of the bar.

"Hey, you bitch, you better shut your mouth before I shut it for you."

I was moving before I even realized. I ripped the shouting man off of the beautiful redhead I had been admiring. As I looked down at him, I realized he was the stumbling drunk from earlier, when I was trying to park.

"I believe the lady said to get lost," I gritted out, barely containing my rage. "Now why don't you scurry off to your frat house before I have to teach you a lesson on how to treat women." I glared down at him until he ran off. I turned my attention to her, needing to make sure that asshole hadn't harmed her. "Are you okay? He didn't hurt you, did he?" I asked. At first she just stared at me, almost in a kind of trance. After a second, she snapped out of it and told me just how fine she was. If I had thought she would be grateful for my interference, I was sorely mistaken. Seeing her up close, I realized that her septum was pierced, and maybe her tongue too. As she was bitching me out, I thought I saw a flash of silver in her mouth, but I wasn't sure. She also had the most beautiful stormy gray eyes I'd ever seen. After getting turned down for her phone number, I walked back to the bar to find Roger looking half amused and half disbelieving.

"That was rough, bro. I thought she definitely would have at least given you her name or a thank-you after that," he said to me.

"Yeah, oh well. At least I got that asshole off of her." I looked at him and held my hand out for him to shake. "Well, it's been good talking to you, Roger. Good luck with everything, and I'm sorry again about your situation." He thanked me for the shot as I paid.

I put my credit card back in my wallet and walked out of the bar. I got into my white Audi and shut the door. I took my phone out, turned on my Alkaline Trio Pandora station, and then pulled into traffic and made my way home.

The next morning, I dragged myself out of bed and over to the coffeepot. I made a stronger pot than usual. I was definitely going to need it. I felt like I had sandpaper coating my eyelids. I looked at the clock. 5:30 a.m. I had to be at the station in an hour. At least today was my Friday. I had the next three days off. I trudged into the bathroom and turned the shower on. I took my boxers off and as soon as steam started filling the room, I got underneath the spray. The hot water pounding on my back, I picked up the shampoo. As I was massaging my head, images of the spitfire from last night flooded my brain. I thought about what she might look like naked, and if she were in here with me right now, all the things I would do to her to make her call out my name. I opened my eyes and looked down at myself. Damn, I was hard as a rock. I guess I would have to take care of that before I got out. It had been months since I'd gotten laid and it seemed my body was finally noticing.

Images of her on her knees in front of me had me stroking myself. Fuck, that felt good. I could only imagine how good it would feel if she actually had her mouth wrapped around me instead of my hand. She would look up at me with a mouth full of my cock and pure heat in her gaze, bobbing her head up and down on me until I hit the back of her throat and was able to feel her swallow around the head of my dick. Then I would tell her to touch herself while she sucked me off. The first touch of her fingers on her clit would have her moaning around my dick, and the vibrations would only amp up my pleasure. I would watch, mesmerized, as her fingers started swirling around and around. Then she would start fingering herself, pumping in and out in time to how she was sucking me. Just a few more strokes and I would come so hard. I would reach down and tug on her nipple as I grabbed a fistful of her hair with my other hand, holding her in place as I thrusted into her mouth. One more tug of her nipple would have her coming and groaning loudly. The sight of her would send me over the edge and shooting down her throat. Fuck. I came so hard, wishing I knew her name so I could call it out as I did. I opened my eyes and was disappointed to find myself all alone.

I finished up my shower and dried off. I dressed quickly in some jeans and a long-sleeved black shirt. I tied my shoulder-length hair up in a bun so it was out of my way and poured myself some coffee in my to-go cup. Ready to go, I grabbed my wallet and keys and went out the door, locking it behind me.

The drive to work was a bitch this morning. So many people. It had gotten ridiculous lately, with everyone moving here after the legalization of marijuana. You couldn't go anywhere now without there being traffic.

I pulled up to work at 6:25. I was five minutes early, even with all the delays. I walked into the station to see all the guys lounging on the couches. There was a big box of donuts in the center of the table. The five guys who were there all had a donut and a cup of coffee in their hands. Everyone looked as exhausted as I felt. It had been a long week. We were short-staffed and it had been crazy busy. Maybe it was the full moon. Things always tended to get a little nuts around then. I grabbed a maple donut and sat down next to Jerry. Jerry was in his fifties, and he had a wife and three kids. He'd also been here for twenty-five years.

"Hey, Jer, you work the night shift or are you just getting on like me?"

"I just got done. I'm gonna head home soon and go to bed so I can hopefully clean some of the house before Martha gets home from work." Jerry's wife, Martha, was a nurse and had been for about twenty years. They both usually worked the same crazy amount of hours. Sometimes they were scheduled at the same time, but mostly Jerry worked the night shift and Martha worked the day shift. Which meant they rarely saw each other, but when they did they tried to have romantic dinners or go out for a date. All of their kids were in their twenties and out of the house so they didn't have to worry about them. "She's been working a lot of hours at the hospital, so she hasn't had time to clean the house or have home-cooked meals. I would like to surprise her."

"Well, good for you, man. I'm sure she really appreciates you doing that stuff for her. I'll have to take notes for when I get married," I teased, winking at him as I went to clock in.

The day flew by in a whirlwind, just like the rest of the week had. There was a call about a five-year-old boy who had gotten his head stuck in a banister. Then there was a call about an accident on 104th and Huron. A girl had been T-boned in the intersection and her car had spun and hit another car only to spin again and crash into a light pole, knocking it over. It was lucky she wasn't able to open her driver's-side door. The wires from the light pole were exposed with her car over it. It could've been bad. She was pretty shaken up, but didn't have anything physically wrong with her. After that, the boys and I were able to grab lunch before we got our next call. On and on it went all day. Our most interesting call had been a group of girlfriends having a "boyfriend bonfire"; the girls burned all the things their ex-boyfriends had bought them. Unfortunately, they decided to have the fire inside the house and it got a little out of control. Needless to say, when the day was over I was very relieved.

When we got back to the station, I headed to the locker room, took a quick shower, and changed back into my street clothes. On my drive home, I contemplated what I was going to do the next day since I finally had some days off. I probably should go grocery shopping and maybe clean my place, but while that was stuff I needed to get done, there was only really one thing that I wanted to do, and that was to get a tattoo. My good friend at work, Phoenix, had mentioned a place where he went to get his done. My usual tattoo artist had moved out of state, and while I had wanted to get one for a long time, I was skeptical about going to see someone new. It was pretty difficult to find a decent artist who didn't charge an arm and a leg. Anyway, my friend had gotten one done recently that I really liked. The style was right up my alley, so I asked for the information. It was a shop called Tit for Tat, and the tattoo was done by a woman named Savannah.

Chapter 3

Savannah

On Monday, I slept in until around 10:30. Jorge finally got me up, whining in my ear about how hungry he was. I reluctantly got out of bed, fed Jorge, and turned the shower on. I was so glad to finally have a day off. As I stripped my shorts and tank top off, images of the night before flashed through my head. Lauren's tattoo, the drunk guy coming on to me, and finally the gorgeous man coming to my rescue. Now that I was sober and not so cranky, I realized that I had probably been pretty rude to him. Oh well, it's not like I'd ever see him again. There were way too many people in the Denver metro area. I got underneath the spray and let the hot water massage my back before I started my normal shower routine. A couple minutes later, feeling a little more awake from the water, I squirted some shampoo into my hand and washed my hair. Guys were so damn lucky. Girls always had way more stuff on their getting ready to-do list than men. After conditioning, I shaved my legs and washed the rest of my body.

I opened the shower curtain and stepped out. As I grabbed my towel, I looked in the mirror at myself. I was getting a little heavier than I was used to, but my boobs had gotten pretty huge, so I wasn't complaining too much. As I looked at my tits, I admired my nipple piercings. I had barbells instead of rings and I really loved them. I had wanted nipple piercings for a long time, but my ex, Greg, never liked them. When we broke up, getting them pierced was one of the first things I did, kind of a big fuck-you to him. No one had seen them other than the piercer, and I couldn't wait to see what kind of a reaction they would get while I was in bed with someone. I wondered what the man from last night would think of them. I could just imagine him looking at my breasts with heat in his eyes, while he ran his fingers over them. His mouth would follow and close over one of the buds as his hand tugged on my opposite nipple. His tongue would be swirling and nipping on the piercing while his other hand made its way down my stomach toward...

Fuck. I got too carried away. My pussy was now throbbing and I knew I wasn't going to be able to concentrate for a while. I finished drying off, though it wasn't an easy task since my body was so sensitive after my little fantasy, and got dressed in some yoga pants and tank top, sans bra. After blowing out my hair, I had a bagel while I debated where I should clean first, and decided the bathroom would be my priority. I turned some tunes on high and got to work. My cleaning music usually consisted of all girl punk rock bands, who most of the time were pretty angry, and, even though I would never admit it, some Britney Spears and Wilson Phillips. "Dig Me Out" by Sleater-Kinney came on, and I belted along as I finished with the bathtub and got up to start on the sink. I cleaned the bathroom and sang for about another half hour before I got to the rest of the apartment, making sure to do the dishes and the litter box as well. It looked like Jorge was very happy about the latter.

After I was finished, I made myself a sandwich and decided to put a movie on. I perused my collection on Vudu, leaning more toward a chick flick. Ten minutes later, I chose *Bridesmaids*. I put it on and settled in with my lunch, laughing my ass off pretty much the whole time. Jorge looked at me weirdly a few times. Great. Even my cat seemed to judge me. When the movie was finished, I cleaned up my lunch mess and left to grab a bottle of wine. I loved getting a little drunk on my days off after I got all my chores done. It was like a reward for being a responsible adult. When I was cashing out at the liquor store, I noticed the cashier staring at my tits. At first I thought he was just being a guy, until I looked down and realized that I hadn't put a bra on under my white tank top. Oops. Oh well. At least I had nice boobs.

I got home and cracked open the bottle, Jorge whining at my feet the whole time. He loved wine. After pouring myself a glass, I held it down to him, let him have a couple licks, then brought it up to my own lips and had a long swallow. Oh, it tasted so good. It was around six o'clock, so I had a little time before I was going to start on dinner. I turned on my Xbox and put in *Left 4 Dead*. In between rounds, I took long drinks of my wine. I loved playing live because I got to be a zombie sometimes, which was the best part of the game.

Two hours later, I was relatively drunk, having finished almost the whole bottle, and I decided to take a bath. I poured the last glass of wine, started filling the bath with nearly scorching-hot water, and undressed. I also added some lavender and honey Epsom salts and lit a candle. Dear God, it smelled so heavenly. I loved my bathroom. It had black-and-white-checkered tiles, soft mint-green walls, and a huge metal sun hanging above the toilet. I also had a claw-foot tub so the water level was pretty high, but it took a while to fill. When it was ready, I sunk down as far as I could, sighing as my body completely relaxed.

After about five or ten minutes, my mind started wandering, and wouldn't you know it, my first thought was about the man in the bar. My thoughts pretty much picked up where they left off this morning, with his hand wandering down toward my pussy as he sucked on my nipples. I pretended that my own hands were his, as my fingers started plucking my nipple and slowly circling my clit. I moaned loudly, the sound echoing off of the bathroom tiles, as I felt the first wave of pleasure hit me. I then pictured myself reaching down to feel his hard, massive cock drop into my hands. I would circle the head of his dick with my thumb, imagining what he tasted like. I would drag his head back to my lips for a kiss. I had a fleeting thought about what his kisses would be like. I think I'd be likely to drown in them, and I would die happy if that were the case. I stuck my fingers inside me and moved my thumb to where my nerves bundled. The water sloshed around me as I pictured his fingers pushing in and out of me as far as they would go. I felt my pleasure mount and I exploded around my fingers, groaning uncontrollably.

After I came back from my fantasy world, I washed up, pulled the drain stopper, and got out to dry off. As I was dressing, I realized that I hadn't eaten dinner, which was probably why I was more drunk than I felt I should be. I opened my fridge, and saw some leftover pasta that I had made a couple of days ago. I turned on the TV as my food was heating up in the microwave. I quickly ate, absently watching whatever I had put on. Finally, I climbed into bed at around 10:30. Jorge once again curled up against my side, purring loudly as I drifted off to sleep.

The next day, I got ready and went into work at noon. It was a Tuesday and I had only one appointment at the end of my shift, so I was assuming that it would be a pretty slow day for me. After setting everything up, I went to the front and chatted with Anna while I put on some music. We were the only two here, and we have a fairly similar taste in music.

About an hour and a half later, I heard the door chime and looked up to greet whoever had come in, only to be stunned into silence. It was the man from the bar! He hadn't seen me yet. Anna greeted him as he said a friendly hello, and then the most surprising words came out of his mouth.

"So, I was referred here by a friend, and I heard that Savannah was really good. I was hoping she was here? I really want to get a tattoo done today."

Oh shit. It just figured that fate would bring this guy in here. In the back of my head I had the thought that my fantasy didn't do him any justice. He was much better looking than I had remembered.

"Yeah, she's actually right here, and she isn't very busy today, so it looks like you're in luck," Anna said, smiling and giggling at him. No doubt she was as affected as I was by his good looks. Reluctantly, I turned to face him all the way, standing and walking over to where he was waiting at the counter. As soon as he realized who I was, I saw surprise and delight flicker through his eyes.

He smiled broadly at me, and said, "Well, wouldn't you know, how nice to see you again, Savannah." His mouth caressed my name in the most delicious way. He had emphasized it, hinting at the fact that he was very glad he now knew my name.

"Oh. Um, yes, you too." I held out my hand to shake his. "I didn't catch your name."

"It's Charlie. Charlie Watson," he said as he grabbed my hand. I immediately felt a tingly warmth spread through my fingers and up my arm. Oh no. I didn't know how I was going to tattoo this man with how strong a reaction I was having to him. Especially if it was on his torso and I had to stare at his, I'm assuming, very sculpted back or chest.

"Well, I'm Savannah Ajax. So, what were you thinking you wanted to do, tattoo wise?" I said, trying my best to be professional.

"I would really love to do a ski lift with some cool ass trees next to it. Probably all in black. I was thinking on my upper arm."

"Yeah, I could do that. Why don't we go over to the computer and see if we can find a design that you at least kind of like and then I can make modifications from there?"

We sat down in front of the computer and I started browsing Google for what he described to me. I was acutely aware of how close we were, and I was having trouble concentrating. After a couple minutes we came across an image that we both seemed to like quite a bit. It had the silhouette of a snowboarder on the lift, there were pine trees on each side of the lift, and it was all in black with a little bit of white and fairly simple. I printed it out so we could talk about what he wanted to keep and what he wanted to change.

"How about we have the lift getting smaller as it goes up and then fading out at the end? I was also thinking that we could have the trunks of the trees almost look like they're bleeding down abstractly, if that makes sense?" I asked him.

"Yeah, I know what you mean. I love that idea. I would also like for there to be lots of highlights in it, almost like rays of sunshine? So we would have, like, the top right be the brightest and have more shading on the lower left-hand side," he said.

"Perfect. I really like that," I said as I got out my tablet and started sketching our new idea. After about a half an hour of fiddling, I stopped and asked Charlie what he thought.

"I love it. It's even better than I was imagining."

"Awesome. Let me just print this stencil out and we can get it started," I said as I hit print. I took the stencil over to my station, feeling Charlie right behind me. He was standing so close; I could feel the heat from his body seeping into my back. "Okay, why don't you take off your shirt so it doesn't get in our way," I said, trying to sound as casual as I could, even though I was finding it hard not to blush as I thought about him shirtless.

"Oh, trying to get me outta my clothes already, huh?" he joked as he winked at me, taking his shirt off.

Holy. Mother. Of. God.

I couldn't take my eyes off of him. He had a six pack and all of the muscles in his torso were perfectly toned. He wasn't body builder type strong, which was always way too much in my opinion, but he was just strong enough to look completely delicious. I'm pretty sure I was drooling. "See something you like?" he asked, and that stupid, all-knowing smile on his face caused a rush of arousal to flood to my nether regions.

I glared at him, my face turning red with embarrassment about being caught. "Just come over here so we can get started," I practically growled.

"Yes, ma'am," he said, chuckling and walking over to me.

I grabbed a razor and some green soap solution, and quickly wiped off his arm before bringing the razor to it. I rested my hand on his shoulder and heard him inhale sharply. I almost moaned out loud before I caught myself. At least he was just as affected as I was. I thought this was going to feel like one of the longest tattoos I'd ever done.

Chapter 4

Charlie

As soon as Savannah touched me, I knew I was done for. I couldn't believe my luck when I walked in and found out that she would be the one tattooing me, and that I finally learned her name. Savannah. It fit her perfectly. I loved her ideas for my ink too. When she finally printed out the stencil, I was pleased by how it all turned out. And then she touched me. I couldn't stop the gasp as she rested her hand on my shoulder to get me ready. I knew she heard it too, because she immediately closed her eyes, as if trying to regroup. It was like a zing of electricity shot through us both at the contact.

A couple minutes later, I was looking in the mirror at the placement as she positioned the table how she wanted it and put on a pair of gloves. It looked perfect and I couldn't wait to have it on me permanently. I smiled and turned to her.

"It's just what I wanted and the placement is great."

"Oh good," she said, motioning for me to come back to her station. "Okay, why don't we get started? Lie on your back and set your arm here." She gestured to the table and the Saran Wrap that lay where my arm was supposed to go as she talked. I did as she asked, making sure to get comfortable. I would probably be here for at least three to four hours. As soon as I was settled, she sat down and picked up her tattoo gun, dipped it in the ink, and looked at me. "Ready?"

"For anything." I looked at her, my expression serious for a moment. She swallowed hard before she turned her attention back to my arm. She set her left hand on my arm while her fingers stretched my skin, the electricity of her touch once again taking me off guard, although it wasn't as strong as last time since she had a glove on, and causing goosebumps to rise across my chest. Her right hand brought the gun to my arm and we got started. I took a moment to appreciate the sound of the tattoo gun when she turned it on. That was always one of my favorite things. Call me weird, but I loved the buzzing hum of all the guns and the smell of blood and ink.

I watched her as she worked, a look of pure concentration on her face, and occasionally her tongue would slip out or she would bite her lip. Every time she did either one, I would grow a little harder. It was taking all my concentration not to let my erection get out of hand. I tried to distract myself with conversation, but every time I heard her sexy, throaty voice, it only made it worse. I also made the mistake of glancing down at her whenever she leaned over, and I got a clear view of her amazing tits spilling out of her top. That made my mouth water and my hard-on become full blown and I almost groaned out loud before clearing my throat to muffle it. Savannah stopped and glanced up at me, and before I could look away, she immediately saw where my eyes were, and then she looked down to my pants where my body was giving away exactly the thoughts I was having.

I saw her eyes widen before she swallowed roughly and quickly moved her attention back to my arm.

"So what do you do, Charlie?" she blurted, obviously trying to steer things back to neutral ground.

"I'm a fireman," I replied.

"Oh really? That's awesome. I bet you've helped out a lot of people." She sounded genuinely impressed, which always made me feel uncomfortable. I loved what I did, and that I was able to help people in need, but I didn't like getting recognition for it. I did my job to save people, not to make myself feel good.

"Yeah, I guess," I said, ready for a subject change. "So, how long have you worked here?"

"I've been here for about a year, but I've been tattooing for about four years, not including my apprenticeship, which was around a year, and I started that when I was twenty."

"Oh wow. So a while then. Sounds like I'm in good hands," I said as I smiled and winked at her, enjoying watching the blush that rose on her cheeks. "Where did you work before this?" I asked.

A strange look crossed her face, but it was gone before I could place it. "I did my apprenticeship at a shop in Fort Collins. I worked there until I started here."

"Why did you move down here?" I asked.

That strange look crossed her face again. This time it lasted a little longer. The majority of it was sadness, along with anger, and maybe regret? "I'd rather not talk about it," she said suddenly. I could tell she felt uncomfortable, and I felt bad about asking stupid questions that made her remember something unpleasant. "Why don't we take a little break? We're about halfway done and I could use a cigarette." She quickly stood up and took her gloves off, walking away before I could answer her.

Well, that was interesting. I was curious as to what set her off. Obviously, it was something related to where she had been working in Fort Collins. Maybe she got fired and left on bad terms? Or maybe there was an ex-boyfriend involved? I continued wondering about it as I got up off the table and headed to the restrooms. After I finished up, I washed my hands and caught a glimpse of myself in the mirror.

I had circles under my eyes from the lack of sleep and from being overworked this last week. My gaze then went to my new tattoo. It was only about halfway done, but I could already tell it was going to look amazing. Savannah really was a fantastic artist. I also glanced at my chest, recalling when I caught her ogling me. I wasn't vain or anything, but I knew I had a nice body. I had to be in shape with my job, otherwise I wouldn't last longer than a couple hours. It still stirred a pleasurable feeling inside of me. I might have even puffed up my chest for a second before I realized what I was doing, and I instead teased her about it a little, loving the blush that instantly showed up on her cheeks. I needed to stop my train of thought. If I kept going, I would start to get hard again, and I had just started to settle down.

When I finally opened the door, I looked around, but didn't see Savannah. It seemed that she was still smoking. I guessed she needed a few minutes to herself, so I let her have it and settled back onto the table to wait for her. About five minutes later, she walked in and washed her hands, seeming quite a bit calmer than when she had gotten up to go outside. She put a new pair of gloves on and smiled at me. Fuck, that smile would be my undoing. It ignited something that I wasn't quite comfortable with.

"Ready to start back up again?" she asked me.

"I am if you are," I replied as I watched her pick the gun up and dip it back in the ink.

"Sorry I darted off so quickly. It had been a couple hours since I had my last cigarette and I was really starting to feel it."

"Oh, no worries. Sorry if my question upset you. I was trying to get to know you a little better," I said, needing to apologize. I really hadn't liked being the one to put that look on her face and make her rush out of the room.

"Oh, it didn't. No need to apologize," she said quickly, even though I could tell she didn't mean it. I decided to let it drop; I was obviously making her uncomfortable again.

"So, how would you feel about going to grab some pizza with me after this?" I asked. Damn. This was probably going to make her uncomfortable too. Way to go, Watson.

"Well, I have another tattoo after you, so I can't," she replied. She actually looked regretful. Maybe there was still hope for me with this girl.

"Well, what time are you off work? I wouldn't mind waiting. I could run some errands while you finish up here."

She considered it for a moment or two. It looked like she was having an internal argument with herself. Finally, "Okay. I'm off at eight. Why don't we meet at the pizza place at around eight thirty? I need to clean up first," she said, smiling at me.

"Okay," I said, smiling back at her.

After that we didn't talk much. She was focused on my tattoo again and I was content just watching her. We were closing in on the four-hour mark, and I could definitely feel it. It looked like she was almost done. She was working on the white, highlighting everything and making it look like the sun was shining down on the whole scene.

She kept innocently brushing her body against mine to get better angles for herself, and it was driving me wild. Every time it happened, the hair on my arm would stand on end. She didn't notice until the very end, and I felt one of her nipples harden under her shirt as she looked up at me. She quickly backed up and cleared her throat before shaking her head slightly.

"Okay, Charlie, just a couple more minutes and we should be done," she said breathlessly. "You hanging in there? This was a little bit longer of a session than some people like to do."

"Yeah, I'm good. I'm getting a little raw, especially when you wipe it, but I'm doing okay," I replied just after she'd wiped it down again. That was always the worst part for me with these longer sessions. By the end, it started feeling like she was wiping my tattoo off with sandpaper.

"Yeah, I get like that too. Sometimes by the end I actually get pretty nauseous," she said while she did her last couple lines. "Okay, I think I'm finished. Why don't you go take a look at it?"

I hopped off the table and walked over to the mirror across the room. I took a minute to look over all the details. It looked so good! I really loved all the shading and highlight work she did. That's what took it from good to great. The stencil just showed the black, and she improvised most of the highlighting, so I didn't know how that part was going to turn out. After I was done examining it, I turned to her. She looked a little nervous for some reason. "I love it, Savannah. You did such a great job. Thank you so much." At my words, she visibly relaxed and gave me a big smile.

"Oh good. I'm so glad. Why don't we head up to the register and get this all taken care of?" she asked as she turned and started walking toward the front of the shop. I of course watched her ass sway as she walked away from me, not able to help myself.

When we got to the desk, she looked at the clock. Like I thought, it had been about four hours. It was a pretty big piece, taking up almost my whole biceps, and believe me, I didn't have small biceps. After she calculated how much it would be, I pulled out my wallet and handed over my card. She swiped it and gave it back to me with a receipt for me to sign, which I did, also adding in about a twenty-five percent tip. Normally, I did only twenty percent, but I was very happy with her work, and I wanted to keep coming back to her.

"So I was thinking we could go to Pizza Alley, it's on 33rd and Lowell. How does that sound?" I asked her, a little nervous that maybe she'd changed her mind.

"Yeah, that sounds good. My next client is supposed to be here in about a half hour, but it's a pretty small piece so it should only take me maybe forty-five minutes. I think by the time I finish with her and clean up, it'll be around 8:30?"

"Okay, that's perfect. Why don't you text me when you're about to leave and I'll head over there?" I asked her as I grabbed a pen and paper, and wrote down my number for her.

"Yeah, that sounds perfect," she said as she smiled down at my number. She was distracted, so I grabbed her hand and brought it to my lips before she could stop me. As I kissed the back of her hand, her eyes snapped back up to mine. I thought I saw heat flashing in her eyes, but I wasn't sure.

"In that case, see you soon, Savannah." I dropped her hand and turned to walk out the door.

Chapter 5

Savannah

I watched Charlie leave, stunned. He left before I had a chance to say anything or react. Smart move. I guess I wouldn't have known how to react anyway. I was trembling just from the innocent act of him brushing his lips across my hand. I wondered how it would feel to have his lips on other parts of me. I squashed that thought down as soon as it popped into my head. This just made me all the more anxious about going out with him later. I was still fighting strong feelings for him, but it was becoming more and more difficult. He probably sensed that from me, and that was why he took off before I could change my mind about tonight.

Anna came up behind me and scared the shit out of me, yelling, "Holy shit! That was hot! Girrrrl, you are lucky! He is so into you!" very loudly right by my ear. "And he was so yummy. I didn't think I was gonna stay upright when he took his shirt off," she said, fanning herself.

"Whatever. Maybe he's like that with all girls. He could just be a total flirt," I said, even though I didn't really believe it myself.

"You are blind, lady. Maybe if tonight goes well, he'll be kissing other parts of your body instead of just your hand," she said as she chuckled, winked at me, and walked off.

What was it with everyone stunning me into silence and then walking off before I could reply? I glanced up at the clock. Shit. My client was going to be here soon, and I still hadn't cleaned up my station from Charlie. I got my ass into gear, wiped everything down, and organized all my tools. I finished just as my next client walked in the door. She was about ten minutes early, which I always loved. I hated having to wait on clients, especially if they were late.

"Hey, Chelsie. How are you?" I asked her as she walked up to the front desk.

"I'm great, Savannah! A little nervous though. I think I told you this when I came in to talk to you the other day, but this is my first tattoo. I'm really excited but still pretty anxious," she said, looking around at everything.

"I totally understand, hun, but don't worry. I will take good care of you. It's good that you're getting a small piece for your first time, that way you can see if you like it, and if it hurts too much for you, you won't be sitting through hours of torture," I said with a laugh. I smiled widely, trying to put her at ease. I then went over to the desk, where I had already printed off the sketch I did for her after she came in for her consultation. It was pretty simple, just a sun on her hip, nothing too complicated. I changed it up a little so it didn't look so generic. I brought the picture over, and showed it to her.

"What do you think? Is this close to what you were picturing?" I asked her.

"Yes, it's great! But there's no color in it. I was hoping we could add some reds and oranges?" she said, looking a little concerned. This was very common with newbies. I got this question all the time. A lot of people didn't understand that I couldn't put color on the stencil; I just have a general idea in my head before we start, and then add to it once I'm done with the outline and all the black.

"Of course. I remember you saying that when you came in. The stencil just always prints black, but I will put some in and make it look awesome. Promise," I said, smiling at her. "Other than that is there anything else you want to change?"

"Nope! I really love the design."

"Perfect. Let me just print the stencil out and then we can get started," I told her, heading over to the computer. As soon as I had it printed, I had her follow me back to my station. I quickly got her skin ready and put the stencil on. Once she was satisfied with the placement, I had her lie down on the table. I could feel the anxiety rolling off of her.

"Don't worry, Chelsie. It really isn't as bad as you're picturing in your head, but if it's too much, just let me know and I'll give you a little break, okay?" I told her, trying to calm her down a little. She nodded and I dipped my gun in the ink, and looked at her. "You ready?"

"Ready as I'll ever be." She took a deep breath and I got started. After about five minutes she started talking. "You were right. This isn't so bad. It was much worse in my head. It still hurts, but not as bad as I thought."

"Yeah, it's usually like that for everyone. I was so nervous for my first one. I didn't eat all day, and by the time I was done with my tattoo, I almost passed out," I told her, trying to distract myself. This tattoo was going by super slow for me, probably because I was anxious to see how tonight was going to go with Charlie.

Thirty minutes after I started, I cleaned her up. She checked it out in the mirror, and then paid. I quickly cleaned my station, and finally texted Charlie that I was just about to leave. I grabbed my purse and said goodbye to Anna before I made my way to my car. Getting in, I quickly lit a cigarette, and took a big drag. Charlie texted me back that he was just pulling up to Pizza Alley. I put my music on, and pulled out onto the street as I tried to power-smoke through my cigarette. I had to drive only a couple blocks away, so I didn't have much time. When

I parked, I got out, only to see Charlie walking over to me with a big smile on his face. He took me off guard when he pulled me into his arms, and kissed my cheek.

"Hey, I'm really glad you decided to come out with me. You ready to head inside? I bet you're hungry after tattooing all day," he said just as my stomach growled loudly. We both laughed as he opened the door for me.

"Yeah, I guess I am pretty hungry," I said, taking him in. He had showered since I last saw him. He also changed into a T-shirt, which partially showed off his new ink. The ink that I had put on him only a few hours ago. The thought was kind of erotic, and I felt heat pooling between my legs the more I looked at it. Tattooing him had been the most delicious torture. The whole time, I had wanted to run my hands over his gorgeous abdomen and chest, and then I had looked down, only to see that he also thought that what we were doing had been just as erotic as I did.

I was distracted from my thoughts as Charlie turned to me, and asked me what kind of pizza I wanted. I blushed at the thoughts that I was having, but I quickly turned to the guy taking our order.

"Just a slice of cheese pizza, extra cheese, please," I said. "Oh, and a side of ranch."

"And I'll get a slice of pepperoni, and a drink, please," Charlie said, taking out his wallet. I pulled mine out too, ready to pay for my meal, but I didn't get very far. "Don't even think about paying. This one's on me," Charlie said, and handed over his credit card before I could get mine out.

"You didn't have to do that. But thank you," I said as we found our seats.

"If it had been over five dollars, I would've made you pay for it, so don't expect it next time," Charlie teased, and I chuckled.

"I was gonna say, you're quite the big spender. You blew me away

34

over there with that major credit card of yours," I said, teasing him right back. A couple minutes later, our names were called to let us know that our food was ready. "I'll go get it," I said, standing up. "Only fair since you paid." I smiled at him as I got our food.

I brought it back to the table, and we dug in. We were silent for a few minutes as we ate, occasionally glancing at each other. It was kind of hot watching each other eat. I'm pretty sure he thought so too. Whenever I would go to take a bite, his eyes would zero in on my mouth, and they would flash with heat until I found myself squirming in my seat. When we were finished, he cleared his throat, and said to me in a husky voice, "So tell me what you like to do. I need a distraction."

"What do you need a distraction from?" I asked him, confused.

"From all the dirty thoughts I'm having after watching that sexy mouth of yours."

"Oh," I said, breathing a little heavy. I liked that he was having those kinds of thoughts about me, even though I probably shouldn't. I barely knew him, but I didn't feel that way. I actually felt really comfortable around him. I would have to be careful about that. "What kinds of dirty thoughts were you having?" I asked him, my voice rough with desire. Surprise flickered across his face.

"Are you sure you want to know?" he asked me. I nodded at him to continue. "I was thinking about how your mouth would look wrapped around my fingers, sucking them while I'm inside you."

I bit my lip and closed my eyes, the vision assaulting me at once. I tried to stop the moan that was coming up my throat, but it was no use. As soon as it escaped, I shook my head, trying to get the image out of my head. I opened my eyes only to meet Charlie's fiery gaze.

"That's a good new fantasy," I whispered.

"New fantasy? You mean there have been old ones?" he asked, sounding excited and surprised.

"I plead the fifth," I said, blushing. I couldn't believe I told him that.

Now he knew that I'd been fantasizing about him.

"Well, there have been old images for me with you too. Want to share yours?" he asked, a twinkle in his eyes. The bastard didn't think I had the lady balls to say!

Oh, he wanted to play it this way, did he? Well, two could play this game.

"In fact, I do. I took a bath yesterday, and as I rubbed my pussy, all I could picture was that it was you stroking my wet flesh, while I ran my hand up and down your hard cock," I said, and I heard his sharp intake of breath. One point for me. There was no way he thought that I would describe my fantasy to him, especially in such detail.

"That's a good new image for me too," he said, his voice like gravel, it was so rough. He reached down and adjusted himself, smiling as he shook his head.

"Hey, guys, sorry but we closed about twenty minutes ago. I hate to kick you out but I've gotta start cleaning up," the clerk said, interrupting our intimate, sexy moment.

"Oh, sorry, man, for some reason I thought you guys were open for a little while longer. We'll get out of your hair," Charlie said as he got up, and started collecting our trash. I stood up to help him. After we tossed our trash, we made our way to the front. Charlie opened the door for me, and we walked into the warm summer night air. We headed in the direction of my car, Charlie guiding me, his hand on my lower back. The warmth and firmness of it sent tingles through my whole body, and I almost moaned out loud at the contact. He suddenly stopped, and I looked back at him, curious why, only to find that we were in front of my car. I had been so distracted by his hand that I didn't notice when we had arrived.

I glanced between him and my car, reluctant for our night to end. I really enjoyed spending time with him. I started walking toward him, only to have him grab my hand, and pull me into his arms. He looked down at me, brushed a stray tendril of hair out of my eyes, and slowly inched his face closer to mine, as if to give me time to change my mind about what I knew he was going to do next. I wanted it just as much as he did, especially after our little conversation about fantasies, so I closed the distance. The first touch of our lips was gentle, just a soft brushing of our mouths. I wrapped my hand around his neck, and fisted my fingers through his hair. I felt his tongue probing my lips, and opened my mouth for him. He growled his approval as our tongues clashed, pulling me close to him, the contact from his hard body making me moan. My nipples were hard as they pressed against his chest. He tasted like pizza, soda, and something that I could see myself becoming addicted to, something that was uniquely Charlie. After a few minutes, he reluctantly pulled away, breathing hard. "You are delicious," Charlie said, "but I'm trying very hard to be a gentleman, so I'm going to say good-night."

"Yeah, okay. I should probably go anyway; I have to work tomorrow," I said, even more reluctant to leave than before. I made my way to my driver's-side door, feeling Charlie right behind me. He opened the door for me, and I climbed in and looked up at him.

"I have the next two days off. Maybe we can get together again before I have to go to work?" he asked me, looking hopeful.

"Um, I'll let you know. I have to work, so I don't know if I'll have time," I said, still fighting my feelings for him. I know we just had a really hot make-out session, but now that his tongue was no longer down my throat, I didn't know if this was such a good idea. I really didn't want to get into a relationship like I was in before, and I didn't know what he was really like. Maybe he was super controlling, or maybe he was secretly abusive. Okay, now I was trying to talk myself out of it. *Ugh!* Why did he have to affect me so? If my attraction to him wasn't so strong, I wouldn't have had this problem.

"Okay, beautiful, well, I'll text you tomorrow. Drive safe, and sleep tight." He leaned in and kissed me. It was probably going to just be a quick goodbye kiss, but of course as soon as his lips touched mine, I opened my mouth for him, and it quickly became a little more passionate. A minute later, I broke off the kiss and said good-night as I started my car. I watched him walk up onto the curb, pulled out of my spot, and waved to him as I drove off.

Chapter 6

Charlie

Fuck, I was in deep. I barely knew this girl, and I already couldn't get her out of my mind. I went home after our kind-of date, took my shirt off, and looked at my tattoo. I was in love with it. It looked so good, but man, did it hurt like a motherfucker now. It had been a long session, and the longer the session, the worse it stung when it was done. I always thought it felt like a horrendous sunburn, especially when it came to the hot water. I should probably wash it again before I went to bed. I went over to the bathroom sink, washed it as quickly as I could with antibacterial soap, and put some Aquaphor on it when I was finished. I looked at the clock; it was almost ten. Still pretty early, but I was exhausted. I undressed, leaving on my boxer briefs, and collapsed on my bed. I was asleep as soon as my head hit the pillow.

I was walking down the street. It was drizzling rain, and by the looks of the sky, it wasn't going to stop anytime soon. All of a sudden, a two-story building down the street caught fire. I started running toward it, prepared to go in and help get everyone out. As I was running, I saw Savannah in the window on the second floor. I ran faster, but I wasn't getting there any quicker. I shouted her name, but she didn't seem to hear me. My feet felt like they were trying to run through mud. The flames started licking higher and higher, up to where Savannah was. When they reached her, she didn't struggle, almost as if she was immobilized, but she did start screaming—a blood-curdling scream. I finally reached the building, and ran up the stairs as fast as I could. The door to the room she was in wouldn't budge, no matter what I did. I pounded and pounded, ran into it with my body, trying to break it down. Still nothing.

"SAVANNAH, LET ME IN! I CAN SAVE YOU!" I screamed, desperate to get to her.

As soon as the words were out of my mouth, the door opened, and there stood Savannah, engulfed in flames, tears streaming down her face, but her face and voice was calm as she said to me, "I don't need you to save me, Charlie," and slammed the door, the force of it sending me tumbling down the stairs and out of the front door just as the building exploded...

I jerked awake, breathing hard. I was covered in sweat, and my heart was pounding. Fuck. I had nightmares like this every now and then, but it was usually the same one over and over. Usually it was my past coming to haunt me, my loved ones dying, and me not being able to save them. I didn't like this new development. Before memories of my past flooded my head, I got out of bed, determined to distract myself from them, and the nightmare. I quickly tended to my tattoo, and got dressed in running shorts, shoes, and nothing else. I grabbed my iPod and some water, and headed out the door. As soon as I got to the street I started jogging. Whenever I had a nightmare, this was what I did, usually to the point where I couldn't move or think after I was done. I looked around—it was 5:00 a.m. so the city was quiet, which was just how I liked it, but it was also dark. I made my way to the park and lake that was about a mile away from my house. I would run laps around that lake until I couldn't move anymore.

An hour later, I was exhausted, but mission accomplished. All I could think about was how bad my muscles were burning. I also couldn't believe how amazing the sunrise was. After my run, I collapsed in the grass next to the lake, and now the sun was coming up, shining on the water perfectly. It was moments like this when I realized how tiny and insignificant everything is. The universe is so small and we are so big. No, wait. Strike that. Reverse it. Thank you, Willy Wonka. But seriously, times like this really put everything in perspective. I've had my fair share of shit, but a lot of people have had a lot worse. Feeling much better, I finished my bottle of water, got up, and headed back to my house.

As soon as I walked in, I went to the bathroom, stripped, and turned on the shower. I stepped in, and let the hot water cascade down my back, relaxing my muscles. When I finished cleaning myself, I stepped out, got dressed, and like normal, put my hair up into a bun. I went to make myself a pot of coffee, exhausted from my nightmare and my early morning run, and thought about what I needed to do that day. I was supposed to clean and go to the grocery store yesterday, but I got too eager about my tattoo, and went in early, then went out with Savannah, so I needed to get both done. My house wasn't too messy; I tried to clean it once a week, but with work being so crazy the week before, it was a little messier than I would've liked. I decided to go to the grocery store first; after all it was seven, so it would be pretty slow. I quickly made a list and ran out the door.

I pulled up to the grocery store, parked, and walked in. As soon as I went to grab a cart, I bumped hands with someone. Realizing that a woman my age and I were going for the same cart, I immediately pulled back.

"I'm sorry. I didn't see you there. You are more than welcome to take this cart, and I'll find another one," I said. The lady giggled and blushed. By the looks of it, she didn't get much male attention, if she was blushing just from me talking to her.

"Oh, you don't need to do that, I was just in a rush, and wasn't looking where I was going. I'm sure you got here first."

"No really. I'm in no hurry today. Please take it."

"Okay, twist my arm," she said, giggling again and batting her eyelashes at me. "Thank you so much." I watched as she walked off with the cart, or more like ran.

I grabbed another cart and started making my way around the store, picking up stuff off my list, but my mind was on Savannah. I wondered if my dream meant anything. I knew that she was an independent woman, she made sure I knew it the night I met her, but I wondered if something happened to make her that way, or if she was just naturally like that. I had a feeling it was the former. She was going to resist me every step of the way, I was sure, but I was going to try my hardest to make her mine. I didn't know what it was about her, but I just couldn't get her out of my mind. Her sass, her resistance, her intelligence, her artistic ability, and, let's be honest, her looks. All of it made for one hell of a sexy woman.

I shook my head, trying to concentrate on the task at hand. An hour and two hundred dollars later, I made my way out to my car, loaded everything in, and headed home. By the time I got everything unloaded and settled, it was 9:00 a.m. I sat there wondering when it would be too early to text Savannah. I should probably wait a couple hours still. That was okay, I still needed to clean, so maybe when I was done with that. I got to work on the house, cleaning all the rooms, and paying special attention to the bathroom. Two hours later, I was all finished. I loved when the house was clean like this. I could breathe easier. I opened all my windows, and decided to make myself a wrap for lunch. As I sat down to eat, I glanced at the clock. Noon. I thought it would be safe to text her now.

Hey, beautiful. How's your day going so far?

I turned the TV on while I ate, and waited for her reply. *Ghost Adventures* was on. This show was cheesy as fuck, but I really liked it. I found the back stories very interesting. This episode was about an actress in the 1930s who committed suicide by jumping off the Hollywood sign. Even though she couldn't be famous acting, she would always be famous for jumping off that fucking sign. Probably why she did it, or at least why she did it the way she did. I finished up my wrap just as I heard my phone chime with a new message.

Pretty good so far, handsome. How about yourself?

Oh, she was flirty today. I liked flirty Savannah. Then again, I liked every version of Savannah so far.

I'm great, except for the fact that I can't seem to get my mind off of this really hot girl I made out with last night ;)

Is that right? She must be one lucky girl. I bet she can't get her mind off of you either.

Do you think this lucky girl would wanna get together soon?

Up until now, her replies were very quick, but after that last text, she took her time getting back to me. Probably debating whether or not it was a good idea. I was just about to text her again to try to convince her, when her reply popped up on my screen.

I'm free tomorrow after 6...

Yes! Now I had the opportunity to take her on a real date. The first one was fun, but I didn't feel like it was technically a date, since it was just going out for pizza. I decided to take her to the Cheesecake Factory in Boulder this time around.

Perfect. Pick you up at 7?

How about I just meet you there?

I would rather pick you up. I want it to be a surprise.

Fine. Pick me up at 7:30.

I smiled to myself as she texted me her address. I knew she was going to fight me every step of the way. This way it felt more like a date, and I could surprise her with the location. Not that it was a "unique" place or anything, but it was a little fancier (which I knew she would object to), and she could get some cheesecake. I wasn't sure, but I had a feeling that Savannah had a major sweet tooth. Maybe if things went well, we could grab a bottle of wine, hang out at my place, and have a chance for something a little more intimate. We had seen each other a couple times now, but we had never had the opportunity to be alone together. I was desperately hoping that if I were to get some real one-on-one time with her, then maybe she would let some of her walls down, and finally get a little comfortable with me.

Suddenly I got another text from her.

What should I wear?

Oh, she was trying to get a hint as to where we were going. Sneaky little thing.

Something sexy ;)

That ought to get her thinking. It gave nothing away, but let her know that she probably shouldn't wear work clothes.

Ugh! You are so frustrating!

You know you like it ;)

She didn't reply, and I knew that the next night was going to be so much fun. I couldn't wait...

Chapter 7

Savannah

I wondered where Charlie was taking me. The suspense was killing me. It was now the day of our date, and I had no idea what I should wear. I looked at my wardrobe and was sorely disappointed. I was getting so sick of my clothes. I really needed to go shopping, but I didn't exactly have the money. Living in Colorado these days was super expensive, and I didn't have a roommate. A lot of the time I debated with myself: no roommate vs. clothes, and no roommate always won. I did, however, just get a new dress on Wish for $12. It took forever to get here, but it was worth the wait. It was sleeveless and black, and it ended just above my knees, with a thick band just below my boobs. It was pretty retro and adorable. Maybe I should go with the "pinup" style tonight. I set the dress out and put my red heels next to it. I had to get ready for work, but I wanted to make sure I had everything set for when I got dressed for my date later.

I put my hair up in a bun, grabbed my purse, and headed out the door. I pulled up to work, making it in before everyone else, opened the shop, and put some music on. I had a full book today, so at least I would be busy until our date tonight. I really hoped that it would go by fast. As I was setting up my station, Anna walked in.

"Hey, bitch! Wanna hang out tonight? We can watch *Grey's Anatomy* and drink two bottles of wine."

"Normally I'd be all over that shit, but I kinda, maybe, sorta have a date." My voice got quiet as I watched the shock on her face and waited for the crazy reaction I knew was about to come. She didn't disappoint.

"Holy shit!" she screamed. "I'm so happy for you! I thought you would never go on a date!"

"Why, thanks. Way to make me feel like a loser."

"Well, sorry, but you are a little bit. I have never seen you even remotely interested in someone since I've known you."

I just rolled my eyes because, honestly, it was true. I always said I was too busy to go out, but most of the time I wasn't. I never went on dates since I moved to Denver. Greg, my last boyfriend of four years, kind of ruined relationships for me. I met him when I started working at the tattoo shop in Fort Collins. I did my apprenticeship under him, and even though he was a great tattoo artist, he was a horrible teacher. I didn't realize until after I left, but he was constantly putting my work down, telling me that my tattoos looked like shit, and that he couldn't believe that I had studied under him. Then one night...

Greg was working late tonight, so I decided to surprise him with some Chinese takeout. We had this delicious little place down the street from our house. Their lo mein was out of this world, so I made sure there were two orders of the noodles, and some egg rolls. I made a quick stop at the liquor store for some wine, and drove over to the shop. When I pulled up, the front lights were off, but I could see that the lights in the back were still on, which was strange. Maybe he got off earlier than he thought. Smiling to myself at the thought, I got out of the car with all my goodies, and went to open the front door, but it was locked. That was weird. He normally didn't lock the door until he left. I was starting to have a sinking feeling in the pit of my stomach.

I pushed the feeling down, pulled my keys out, and unlocked the door. As soon as I opened it, I heard rustling or something in the back. It sounded like he was cleaning up, so I had come at the perfect time. As I walked to the back, I heard moaning, and I knew what I was going to see before I walked in. I rounded the corner into his room, and I saw Greg lying on his back on the table. On top of him was a naked blonde, riding him, her huge tits flopping all over, and her moans were getting louder and louder. I knew what was coming next but I couldn't look away. Amazingly enough, they still hadn't noticed me. In the next moment, she screamed loudly, and slowed her movements just as I heard Greg groan.

Feeling sick to my stomach, I turned around, set the food on the front counter, and walked out, taking the wine with me. I knew I would need it. I rushed home and started getting all of my shit together. I didn't care if I forgot stuff, or if my packing was messy, I just wanted to get the hell out of there before Greg got home. When I was loading the last bag into my car, I saw Greg pull up and I groaned. I had barely been holding it together while I packed up all my shit, probably because I was kind of in shock, but now that I had to face him, I didn't think I would be able to.

Greg got out of his car, the anger on his face evident.

"What the fuck do you think you're doing, Savannah?" he asked me. I guess he hadn't seen the Chinese food on the counter before he left.

"What does it look like?! I'm fucking leaving! I saw you and that blonde bitch fucking on your tattoo table," I yelled, my voice slightly trembling. It felt good to finally yell at him. In all the time we had been together, I had never once raised my voice to him. My mother had always told me that if I wanted to keep a man, I needed to be the perfect woman, and never disagree with him. So much for that.

"Well, what did you expect? You never satisfy me, you aren't loud enough, aren't willing to try new things, and every time I try to put it in your ass you push me away. I wanted to have every piece of you and you couldn't even give me that. Of course I would start looking for something else," he sneered

at me.

"How do I not satisfy you? I've always done everything you've ever asked, always have sex whenever you want, except the whole anal thing, and that's because you're always too rough. But still, I would never be okay with you cheating, even if I was a terrible girlfriend!" I yelled. God, he was such an asshole. How had I never seen it before? "Also, I wasn't loud because you are horrible in bed. I bet that skanky blonde bitch from earlier was faking it the whole time. Have fun with her, and make sure to get tested, 'cause she looked like she'd been around with some nasty ass guys. You'll never see me again." Before he had a chance to say anything else, I got in my car, slammed the door, drove off, and didn't look back...

"Savannah?" Anna said, snapping me out of my memories. "Are you okay? You know I was just teasing you, right?" She looked concerned.

"Oh, I'm fine. Sorry, I was just thinking of something. I know you were just teasing me," I said, forcing a smile onto my face. I didn't want to make her feel bad. "It's true anyway."

"Okay," she said, looking skeptical. "If you're sure. So, where is he taking you tonight?"

"He won't tell me! I'm so frustrated. He said to 'wear something sexy.' What the fuck does that mean?" Anna laughed at my frustration.

"I would wear a dress or something in case he takes you out to a fancier place. That way it's kind of in the middle. Plus, you can never go wrong with a little black dress."

"Yeah, that's what I was thinking. I decided to go for a kind of pinup style. That's sexy enough, right?" I asked.

"Oooh, that's a great idea!" she exclaimed.

Our conversation was interrupted when my client walked in. The rest of the day passed in a blur. Before I knew it, I had finished up with my last client, and it was 5:45. I quickly cleaned up and said goodbye to Anna before heading out the door. I walked into my apartment at 6:15 and started getting ready, making sure to blare some fun music while I was at it. I picked out some black lace panties and a matching bra, just in case, and put them on as well as my dress while my curling iron was heating up. As for makeup, I decided to go with a smokey-eye look and dark red lips. For the hair, I quickly curled my long locks and twisted my bangs into a pin curl. An hour later, I was ready to go. I put my heels on, and decided to have a quick glass of wine to relax myself before he arrived.

At 7:29 I heard a knock on my door. Right on time. I finished off the rest of my wine, and opened the door. At first, all I saw was a huge bouquet of red roses, until Charlie poked his head around them to look at me.

"These are for you," he said as he handed me the flowers, leaning in to kiss me on the cheek. "You look beautiful, Savannah."

"Thank you," I said, blushing. I wasn't used to men telling me these types of things. Charlie was definitely a gentleman. "Let me just put these in some water before we go."

I walked into the kitchen, feeling Charlie right behind me. I opened my cupboard, and pulled out a vase, quickly filled it, and put the roses in. I left it on my countertop, and turned to face him, finally able to fully look at him. He looked so handsome. He was wearing a black pin-striped button-up shirt with dark jeans, and he had the first button of his shirt undone, just enough for a peek of his gorgeous chest underneath. This was the first time I had seen him with his hair down. It was a little longer than his shoulders and it had a bit of a wave to it. I looked at his emerald-green eyes, and they were hungrily eating me up. He took a step toward me, and brushed a stray tendril of hair out of my face.

"It's going to be hard to control myself tonight with you looking like that," he said, his voice husky, and I swallowed hard.

"What if I don't want you to control yourself?" I asked, my voice rough.

He took a deep breath, closed his eyes, and shook his head. "Come on, you little temptress," he said, taking my hand, and leading me out of the apartment.

"So, are you going to tell me where you're taking me?" I asked as I locked my door.

"Now, what would be the fun in that?" he said, a teasing glint in his eye.

"You are so frustrating! I've been obsessing over it all day!" I said, glaring at him.

He chuckled. "Okay, fine, I'm taking you to the Cheesecake Factory on Pearl St. in Boulder. I have a feeling you like sweets," he said, smiling at me.

"Ooh, yum! I love Cheesecake! And I haven't been to Boulder in a while," I said as he led me down the stairs, his hand on my lower back.

"Good. I thought you might have a sweet tooth. Plus, since it's so nice out, I bet there'll be some street performers."

"Oh, I bet there will be! I love watching street performers. One time, me and my high school friend, Danielle, spent all day on Pearl St., and there were two people playing xylophones, they were so good. We probably spent at least an hour watching them," I said.

Sometimes I missed high school. I feel like it was so much simpler. All I had to worry about was school and work.

"That sounds like fun. I feel like most people think xylophones are just for people in elementary school, but if you really work on it, you can do some really cool things with them."

"Oh for sure. The two of them were so good," I said as he opened the car door for me. I climbed in and then watched him walk around the car and get in. I couldn't help but watch him move; it was so sexy. The way he held his body, the way he walked. He glanced over at me, once again giving me a knowing smile, like he knew what I was thinking. He reached across the console and grabbed my hand, sending tingles up my arm and butterflies through my stomach. It was going to be a long night...

Chapter 8

Charlie

This was going to be a long night. Savannah looked so fucking delicious. I was trying to be a gentleman, but she was making that very difficult for me. I couldn't keep my hands off of her. I grabbed her hand as I got in the car, and it was so soft and warm. I wondered how it would feel wrapped around my dick. Damn it! I needed to get my mind out of the gutter. I pulled onto the street and headed toward highway 36, noting that there luckily wasn't much traffic. I had Three Days Grace playing in the background as we drove.

"I love this band. I started listening to them back in high school," Savannah said, headbanging slightly.

"Yeah, I love them too. I've always wanted to see them live, but I've never been able to," I replied, weaving in and out of traffic.

"Yeah, same here. I love going to live shows, but I don't get to go too often. I think the last one I was able to go to was The Ghost Inside. They opened for Parkway Drive at the Gothic, it was so amazing, but that was probably about a year or so ago." No way was she a hardcore girl. I didn't think it was possible, but I fell for her just a little bit more.

"You like The Ghost Inside?" I asked, still completely surprised. "I went to go see them at the Marquis a couple years ago. I love them."

"Well, maybe we can go to a show together soon? I think Bring Me the Horizon is coming to the Bluebird next month," she asked, looking slightly vulnerable.

"I would love to go. I've never listened to them before, but it sounds like we have a very similar taste in music, so I trust you," I said, turning to smile at her.

She blushed before saying a simple "Okay."

By this time we were pulling into Boulder; it had been only about a twenty-five minute drive here, which was pretty good considering the area we were in. I found a parking garage a couple blocks down from the restaurant.

"Are you going to be okay walking a little bit in those heels?" I asked, looking down at her feet, subtly admiring her calves on the way there. By her expression, I wasn't as subtle as I'd hoped.

"Yeah, I'll be fine. The last time I wore these, I was a bridesmaid in a wedding, which included standing up front for the ceremony and then dancing in them all night, so I think I can handle a couple blocks," she teased, proceeding to get out of the car and walk toward the stairs with a little sway in her hips. Meanwhile, I was still sitting in my seat, staring after her, unable to move. She turned back, giving me a knowing smile. I shook my head, chuckling while I got out of the car, and made my way over to her. "See something you like, stud?" she asked, giving my words back to me.

"I absolutely do. You are so beautiful," I said, brushing her hair out of her face, the moment suddenly turning serious. "Sometimes when I look at you, I forget to breathe."

I heard her sharp intake of breath as her eyes snapped to mine. I could see her mind working furiously as she thoroughly searched my eyes, maybe trying to figure out if I was just giving her a line, or if I was really serious. I was very serious. She finally looked down, avoiding my eyes. I could tell she wasn't used to receiving compliments. I would have to change that.

"You ready to eat?" I asked, deciding to change the subject.

"Yes, I'm starving." She smiled at me, clearly relieved that I didn't push her on it.

We made our way to the restaurant, my hand at her lower back. It was a beautiful night. It was seventy degrees out and the sky was clear. We walked down Pearl St., and as predicted, there were lots of street performers out.

"What do you think? Do you wanna eat first, or watch some of the performers?" I asked her.

"I'm pretty hungry. I think I would like to eat first."

"Okay, I think I can handle that," I said, smiling at her.

We walked into the restaurant, and were sat right away. Our booth was in the corner of the place, so we had our privacy, which was nice. The server came up to us, and his eyes immediately went to Savannah, not that I could blame him, she looked gorgeous tonight.

"What can I get you to drink tonight?" he asked, his eyes wandering down to her chest.

"I'll just have a glass of the house red, please," she said sweetly, not even looking at him, much to his disappointment.

"And I'll just have a Heineken," I said as his gaze was reluctantly torn from Savannah.

"All right, guys, I'll be right back with that for you."

We were quiet for a few minutes as we looked over the menu. I watched as she skated her eyes over it, looking a little worried.

"Don't worry about prices, beautiful, you can get whatever you want," I told her. She looked skeptical, but returned to reading. "Do you like calamari? Theirs is really good, and I was thinking we could split it if you wanted?"

"Yeah, I love calamari," she said, smiling at me. "What are you going to get for dinner?"

"I pretty much always get the fettuccini alfredo. It's my favorite."

"Ooh that sounds good. I must have missed that," she said as she flipped the page, looking for the pasta section.

"Well, if you decide you want something else, you can always have some of mine," I said. "I'll even feed it to you, if you want."

"You just want an opportunity to stick something of yours in my mouth," she teased. The image immediately brought me back to my fantasy from the shower, and I had to concentrate to keep my breathing under control. Just as I was about to tell her how much I would love to have a certain thing of mine in her beautiful mouth, the server arrived with our drinks.

"Here's your drink, honey. And if you need anything else at all, you just let me know," the server said, making sure to emphasize the *anything*. Savannah caught his obvious flirtation this time, and simply arched an eyebrow at him as he walked away.

"Well, that was awkward. I've never had anyone be that openly flirtatious with me while I'm on a date. What a tool."

I smiled at her obvious discomfort.

"Well, I don't blame him. You look gorgeous tonight," I said, sweeping my gaze over her.

She blushed and said, "You don't look so bad yourself, handsome." Her eyes moved to my chest where I had the top button undone. She bit her lip and made her way down to my abdomen, which I assumed she was remembering from when she gave me my tattoo.

"You can't look at me like that right now, otherwise I won't be able to make it through dinner," I said, my voice rough.

"Oh. Sorry. I didn't realize I was doing it," she said quietly, averting her gaze.

"Hey," I said, her eyes to shooting up to mine, "I love that you look at me like that. I just want to do things to you when you have desire written all over your face from thinking about me, and we really aren't in the place to do anything about it right now. Please, don't be sorry." I smiled at her, wanting to put her at ease. "So what are you gonna get?"

"I think I'm going to get the four-cheese pasta. In case you haven't noticed, I love cheese," she said, taking a sip of her wine.

"Me too. I don't trust people that don't like cheese."

"There are people out there that don't like cheese?! How does that even happen?" she asked.

Just then, the server came back to take our order.

"Can we have the calamari to start, and then I'll have the fettuccini alfredo, and the lady will have the four-cheese pasta, please," I said, ordering for the both of us.

"Okay. I will put your order in right away, and the calamari should be up for you guys soon," he said, his eyes still lingering on Savannah, seemingly disappointed he didn't have a chance to interact with her again.

While we waited for our food, we continued chatting about music. Savannah liked to play the desert island game (if you were stuck on a desert island for the rest of your life, what would be your top five…). We played this after the calamari arrived with music, movies, books, food, and anything else you could think of. It was a great "get to know you" game, and it showed us how much we actually had in common. We had the same taste in music, most movies, and food. The only thing we differed on was books. While pretty much the only books I read were autobiographies, Savannah was a typical woman, and liked smutty romance novels, although she was reluctant to admit it.

Our food finally arrived, and we dug in. After a couple minutes, I twirled some pasta around my fork and held it in front of Savannah. She leaned forward, and closed her lips around my fork, pulling the pasta free. She closed her eyes, and moaned as she chewed. I couldn't help the groan that escaped my mouth. Her eyes snapped open and shot to mine.

"Wanna try mine?" she asked quietly. I nodded and opened my mouth for her. She held out some pasta on her fork, and I watched her as I ate. I swallowed and licked my lips as she watched my every move, heat flaring behind her eyes. "I bet you can do wicked things with that mouth of yours," she said quietly, her breath coming a little faster.

"I guess you'll just have to wait and see. Maybe if you're lucky, you'll find out tonight." My mouth started watering at the thought of tasting her sweet flesh, and I growled.

"I thought you were gonna try to be a gentleman tonight?" she teased.

"I am trying, I'm just not being very successful," I said.

She turned serious for a moment. "Charlie, you are a gentleman. More so than anyone else I've met. Just because you want to act on the attraction between us doesn't mean you aren't one." She then looked as if she was debating telling me something. "Besides, I'm not looking for anything serious, so I don't need you to be a gentleman."

I thought about that for a moment, and realized she was right. She had been giving me signals all night that she wanted me as much as I wanted her. I was trying to back off so that she wouldn't feel like I just wanted sex from her, but from the sounds of it, she didn't feel like that at all, and wouldn't mind if I did (which I didn't like). Just as I was about to address how I felt about it, she spoke again.

"It actually makes me very happy that you think I'm sexy and are so vocal about it. It almost makes me believe that I am beautiful," she said quietly, not quite meeting my eyes. I realized yet again that her previous relationships had been very detrimental to her self-esteem, and were still affecting her, and that was probably the reason why she wanted only a fuck buddy. I reiterated to myself that I really needed to try to help her change her view of herself, and to give her as many compliments as I could.

"Savannah," I said, needing her to look at me and see how much I meant what I was about to say. "You *are* beautiful, and not just on the outside. The more I get to know you, the more beautiful you become to me. Whatever the assholes in your past have said to make you think that you aren't, believe me, none of it's true. My guess is that they saw how sexy and strong you are, and that intimidated them. They couldn't handle that, and so they brought you down instead."

"I've never thought of it that way," she said quietly. "But whatever the reason, it had the same outcome. But let's talk about something else. Why did you become a firefighter?" she asked.

Damn. I knew she was going to ask at some point.

Chapter 9

Savannah

I was tired of talking about this. He had brought up some good points, but it had taken years to break down my self-esteem. It wasn't just going to magically come back because Charlie said some nice things to me. So, I changed the subject, but was immediately sorry I did when Charlie's face changed from tender and affectionate to closed-off and regretful. He cleared his throat before talking.

"Well, it's kind of a tough story, but I'll tell you if you really want to hear it."

"You don't have to tell me, Charlie, if you don't feel comfortable. But if you do, I would like to hear it," I said, trying to make sure he didn't feel pressured into sharing something he didn't want to, especially on our first official date.

"Well, when I was nine, my friend invited me over to his house for a sleepover. My parents let me go, deciding to have a pizza night at home with my younger brother, Timmy." He took a deep breath, a frown marring his gorgeous face. "The next day, I was supposed to be home by ten, but I wanted to stay longer, so I told my friend's parents I didn't need to be home until eleven. As they turned onto my street to drop me off, the first thing I saw was the flashing lights on the fire truck." He stopped talking for a minute. I had a good idea about what he was going to say next, but I hoped I was wrong. When he spoke again, his voice was pained. "Right after 10:00 a.m., a fire started in Timmy's bedroom. They found a candle, and were pretty sure it was the cause of the fire. My parents must have still been sleeping or something, because no one got out. They were all burned alive, and I wasn't there to help them. And I would have been, if I hadn't been so fucking selfish." I gulped my wine trying to keep from crying.

I reached across the table to grab his hand. "Ooh Charlie, I am so sorry. I can't imagine how hard that was for you. And at such a young age too. But you have to know that what happened was not your fault. And if you had been there, you probably would have died in that fire right along with them. You cannot blame yourself, and if they were alive today, I'm sure they would tell you the exact same thing."

"I know. Everyone has told me that for years, but I still feel guilty, you know? I don't think anything will ever change that." He took a big pull from his beer. "But anyway, I decided to become a firefighter to help as many people that were in their situation as I could. I also want to make them proud, and make up for not being there when I should've been," he finished quietly.

"Well, I think that's very big of you. And you know, maybe if that hadn't happened, you wouldn't have become a firefighter, and someone else wouldn't have survived because you wouldn't have been there to help them," I said and saw his expression change.

"You know, I've never thought of it that way before. Thank you, Savannah. That makes me feel a little bit better," Charlie said, smiling at me. "But let's change the subject, huh? I think we've had enough serious talk for tonight. Do you want to share a dessert, or do you want your own?"

I looked at the dessert menu and was taken aback at how many different kinds of cheesecake they had here. I couldn't decide which one to choose.

"There are so many! I think I'm debating between the Kahlua cocoa coffee cheesecake and the carrot cake cheesecake."

"Well, how about we get one of each and split them?"

"That sounds perfect. If I don't end up eating them both on my own," I said, chuckling and only half joking.

"As long as I get to try them both, you can have as much as you want."

As if the server heard us, which he might've, considering how much he had been hitting on me all night, he came up and cleared our plates.

"Did you guys save room for dessert?"

Charlie answered for me again, and our sweets were quickly brought out. I moaned as the first bite hit my tongue. They were both delicious, but I think I liked the carrot cake one just a little bit more. Charlie and I devoured both of them in a short amount of time, and when we were finished, Charlie paid the bill and we headed out.

It had cooled down a bit, not uncomfortably, but as we started walking I got a little chilly, since I hadn't brought a sweater. Charlie noticed my goosebumps as we came across a couple with a guitar and a steel drum playing reggae music. I stopped to let him know that I'd like to listen.

"You look cold. Let me warm you up a bit," Charlie said as he put his arm around me, pulling me in close. After a minute, his warmth seeped into me, and I was able to relax and enjoy the music. The reggae couple was good, playing lots of Bob Marley and other stuff that I didn't recognize. They both had wonderful voices, and they harmonized well together. We stayed to watch them for about a half an hour, and even though it wasn't a long time, I was really ready to go. Charlie had kept me close the whole time, and had been rubbing little circles on my arm, and occasionally up my neck and into my hair. I don't know if his intention was to drive me crazy, but that's what he did. Whenever his fingers would reach the nape of my neck, I'd imagine how his strong hands would feel grasping my hair and pulling firmly, and I almost moaned out loud at the image. The feel of his hard body pressing into mine also had me very aroused. I had my hand against his chest, keeping me steady, and I could feel the definition of his muscles leaving a hot imprint. By the time we were ready to leave, I was drenched and practically squirming.

"Do you want to look for other performers, or are you ready for me to take you home?" Charlie asked, whispering into my ear, the feel of his hot breath on my neck only making me hotter for him.

"I want you to take me home. I have an unopened bottle of wine that you are going to split with me," I said, not giving him the option to say no. I wanted him, and I didn't want to hear the "gentleman" excuse.

He swallowed hard before nodding at me, and directing me quickly to the car. He opened the door for me again before climbing in on his own side. He plugged his phone in, and started some music before pulling out of the space. The man's voice was beautiful as he sang about regrets and moving on.

"Who is this?" I asked. "I love his sound. His voice is so raw."

"This is Emarosa. They are one of my favorites, and a big part of why is his voice," Charlie said.

We made small talk on the drive back, but the tension between us was building and building. I was afraid it was going to reach a breaking point before we got back to my apartment. I unlocked my door, and we were immediately greeted by the smell of the flowers he left me, and by Jorge meowing by his food dish.

"Okay, Jorge, I'll feed you in just a sec!" I exclaimed, slightly exasperated. "Sorry, my cat's a fat ass and has to be fed the second I walk through the door. Why don't you go have a seat on the couch while I feed him and get us some wine?"

I went into the kitchen, quickly fed my fat cat, opened up the bottle of wine, and poured two glasses. I grabbed my Bluetooth speaker, and connected my phone so we could have a little music. I brought everything into the living room, only to see Charlie on the couch petting a purring Jorge on his lap.

"I think my cat has a crush on you," I said, giggling.

"Hey now, we have a bromance. You chicks just don't get it."

"You men and your bromances," I said, chuckling as I handed him a glass of wine and sat down next to him. I grabbed my phone and turned on Lana Del Rey. We both took a big gulp of our wine, our eyes locking.

"Savannah, I can't tell you how fucking stunning you are," he said, leaning a little closer and running his fingers across my cheek. I involuntarily leaned into his touch, closing my eyes.

In the next moment, I felt his lips softly brushing over mine. I sighed in delight and immediately deepened the kiss, blindly setting my wineglass on the table and twining my arms around his neck. I felt Charlie's tongue seeking mine out as we fought for control over the kiss. Within minutes, our original brushing of lips had escalated to a passionate melding of our mouths, both of us breathing hard and clutching each other as if we hadn't been kissed in years. Charlie's hands gripped my waist and pulled me closer even as I raised myself up and into his lap, straddling him. I felt more than heard the growl deep in his throat as I ground against the hard length pressing against my aching core.

I broke the kiss as I fought for air, the moment so intense that I needed a break, but that didn't slow Charlie down. His lips immediately traveled to my neck, one hand tangling in my hair to hold my head at the right angle, and the other at my lower back, pulling me impossibly closer. Charlie slowly started nibbling a path to my ear. He was breathing hard as he sucked my earlobe into his hot mouth, causing a whimper to escape my lips.

He groaned as he whispered, "God, you make the sexiest little noises. They make me so hard." He ground against me, just to show me how hard he really was. "I was having such a rough time while you were eating your dessert. Having to watch those perfect lips wrap around that fork, only for you moan with every bite you took and then lick your lips after. I nearly came just watching you."

"Oh God, Charlie. I need you to touch me. Now."

"All in good time, baby. All in good time," he said, chuckling when I groaned in frustration. One of his hands gripped my hair as he led my mouth back to his, his tongue immediately coming out to trace my lips. I opened my mouth to his invading tongue as I continued to rock against him. I sucked his lip in between my teeth and bit down as I tugged, then licked away the hurt. He groaned against my mouth as his hips involuntarily jerked upward against me.

I could see what he meant by sexy noises affecting him. Every moan or growl from his lips made me impossibly wetter, and made me want to do whatever it was that made him make those noises over and over, just so I could hear them again. I was so turned on that I was pretty sure there was going to be a spot on his pants from how drenched I was, but I didn't care. I just wanted him to touch me. I felt like I was going to combust.

I had finally had enough. I grabbed his hands from around my waist, and put them on my tits. He chuckled at first, but the laugh died in his throat as I thrust against him again, his grip on my breasts tightening. I moved my hands to his chest, and began unbuttoning his shirt, but it was difficult with my hands trembling. When I finally got it undone, I broke the kiss and looked down at what I revealed. Just as delicious as I remembered. I ran my hands over his chest and I heard him inhale sharply. As I trailed my hands down to his abdomen, I felt his stomach muscles jump beneath my touch. I was just getting to his belt when he stopped my hands. I knew he wanted to take this slower, but I couldn't.

I was burning up and only he could put out the flame.

I stood quickly, took a big gulp of my wine, and looked at him as I slowly unzipped my dress. He maintained eye contact with me until the dress dropped and he couldn't hold it any longer. His gaze swept over me, taking in my black lace panties and bra. Before he could stop me, I reached back and unhooked my bra, letting it fall to the ground.

"Oh God, Savannah. You are so beautif—wait, are you pierced?!" He pulled me forward until I was standing directly in front of him, and his face was even with my breasts. "Fuuuuck," he said as his hand hovered over my chest. He quickly glanced up at me, silently asking for permission. I gave a subtle nod and then his fingertips were brushing over me. I hoped he would go straight for the nipple, but he surprised me, starting just on the underside of my breast, then sweeping around the outside and back down right before his whole hand closed over it. His other hand came up and grazed over my other nipple before he took it into his hot mouth. I cried out as he sucked hard and gently bit down on my hot flesh. I heard my piercing hit his teeth and thought the noise was unbelievably sexy. His other hand started tweaking and pulling on my opposite nipple. After a minute or two, he switched breasts and I was a writhing mess. My hands clutched in his hair as I moaned incoherently.

"Charlie, please," I begged him. What for, I wasn't sure, but I was going crazy.

"I know, baby, I know. I'll take care of you," he said as he pulled me down to lie on the couch. He was instantly on top of me, covering my mouth with his, one hand supporting him, while the other started tracing my collarbone. He slowly dragged it down and circled my nipple again before heading lower. By the time he reached my abdomen, I was squirming. His fingers slowly dipped into the front of my panties and he groaned, "Fuck, you're bare."

"I wax," I said, looking up at him. His eyes were on fire for me, and I loved that I could make him look like that. It made me feel powerful. "And not just there. I get it all waxed. Brazilian, baby," I said, winking at him. That seemed to do it because in the next breath, he growled and pulled my panties off. As soon as they hit the floor, his eyes were on me. His fingers followed, tracing every inch of my pelvis before finally dragging through the lips of my pussy. I gasped as he hit my center, swirling his finger around for just a second before he moved on. I didn't have any time to be disappointed though, because in the next moment, his finger was pushing into me. I cried out as his finger curled inside me in a come-hither motion. His mouth finally returned to my chest as his fingers continued to work their magic. My fingers entwined in his hair, holding his head to my breast. He gently bit down before looking up at me.

"I need to taste you, baby," he said, slightly breathless.

"Yes, please. Make me come, Charlie. I'm burning up," I begged. It was all the permission he needed as he worked his way down my body, his tongue then making a slow lick through my drenched cunt. I felt more than heard his groan, and it only added to my pleasure. Then his mouth closed over my clit, and I lost all rational thought. I was too distracted to realize his hands were making their way toward my breasts until he was squeezing and teasing my nipples. I was building and building and I knew I wouldn't last much longer. His tongue swirled around and around, tracing every inch of my flesh before plunging inside me. Just as I was about to come, I felt his beard scratch against my pussy lips and two fingers slip into me and I detonated, calling out his name as I came.

Chapter 10

Charlie

Watching Savannah come was the most beautiful thing I'd ever seen. Her whole face transformed into pure ecstasy and it was a huge ego boost to know that I was the reason why. I continued sucking on her until she relaxed and stopped shaking. After a few moments, she opened her eyes, looking down at me, a blush reddening her cheeks.

"Hi," she said shyly.

"Hi, gorgeous. How are you feeling?"

"So great. But I would feel better if you were inside of me," she said, grabbing me through my pants. I couldn't help the groan that escaped my lips. "And you are not going to stop now," she said, grasping my length harder and moving her hand up and down. "I want you in my mouth and then I want this thick, hard cock inside me."

She pushed against my chest for me to lie down, and wasted no time crawling down my body, unbuckling my belt. I lifted my hips as she tugged my pants and boxers down my legs, and I heard her sharp inhale as my dick sprang free. She licked her lips as she slowly stroked me from root to tip, swirling my precum around the head with her thumb. She then lowered her head, her tongue taking the same path as her thumb, before she sucked me into her mouth. My hand immediately went into her hair, guiding her head to take me how I wanted. After about a minute of her sucking and licking, I couldn't take it anymore. I pulled her up my body and crushed my lips to hers. I fingered her sweet cunt for a minute to make sure she was ready to take me. Once I was satisfied and she was drenched, I broke the kiss and reached in my wallet for a condom.

I held the wrapper up to her mouth, waiting for her to bite down so I could tear it open. I quickly slid the condom on, and positioned myself at her entrance. I looked into her eyes as I guided her hips down and slowly entered her. Savannah's eyes rolled back as we both collectively groaned.

"Fuck, baby. You are so tight," I said as soon as I was balls deep inside of her. I held her still for a moment to let her adjust to my size. "I don't think I'm going to last long."

"I won't either," she said as she started moving. "Fuck, Charlie. I don't think I've ever felt this full before." I groaned at her declaration. She wasn't moving fast enough for me, so I sat up and rotated so that my back was leaning against the cushions, and I grabbed her roughly by the hair to hold her in place as I pounded upward into her. At first I was worried that I was being a little too rough with her, but as soon as I heard her enthusiastic moan, I knew she liked it. I bent my head and snatched her nipple in my mouth, sucking and biting gently. "Harder, Charlie. Harder," she begged, almost incoherently. I didn't know what she wanted harder, so I did all of them, pulling her hair, biting her nipple, and pounding harder into her, which caused her to half moan, half scream, and her pussy to clench around me.

"Savannah, baby, I'm close," I said. I was about to go off, but I wanted her to come with me. I reached down between us, frantically rubbed at her clit, and sucked her tit deep into my mouth, flicking it rapidly with my tongue. She rode me faster, and I could feel my orgasm at the base of my spine. "Come for me. Come all over my dick," I groaned in her ear. Seconds later I felt her release as she spasmed around me, drenching my cock and screaming my name. "Thank God," I said as I finally detonated and thrust deep inside her once more, before I held her still against me, breathing deeply.

I stroked her hair and back as we caught our breath. After a minute or two she sat up and smiled at me. "Well, that was fun," she said, and I chuckled.

"I think *fun* is a bit of an understatement. That was fucking incredible," I said as she slowly started getting up. I bit back a groan as I slipped out of her.

"I'll be right back." She grabbed her clothes and left me sitting alone in the living room. I heard the bathroom door shut a second later. I reached over and grabbed my wine and took a grateful drink before I removed the condom, knotting it at the end.

As I started dressing, I looked around her living room, taking in my surroundings. There were little lantern lights all around the top of the wall, giving the space a soft and romantic glow. She had a dark antique coffee table that I'm guessing she got at a flea market, and her couch was kind of antique-looking too and was a plum color. She had lots of unique things on her walls, but one of my favorites was a bohemian-style cloth tapestry. It was red, orange, and purple and had a huge mandala on it. It seemed that Savannah really liked the bohemian style, and I was sure that if I ever made it into her bedroom that it wouldn't be much different.

Savannah emerged a minute later, her hair up in a messy bun, and big black-framed glasses on her face. She was also wearing little black shorts and a white tank top. She looked so sexy that I was struggling not to get hard again looking at her. Her legs went on for miles and I could see just a hint of her nipple piercings through her tank top. She plopped down on the couch next to me and reached for her wine, taking a long drink of it before leaning back with her glass. She seemed shy and distant all of the sudden. I guess I wasn't too surprised, but I was disappointed.

"Can I see you again soon?" I asked her, hoping that she wouldn't shut me out again after everything that happened tonight.

"Well, I have to work a lot this next week, so I don't know when I will be free again," she said, not meeting my eyes.

I could tell she needed some space, so all I said was an easy "Okay."

I quickly finished up the wine that she poured me earlier. When my glass was empty, I stood and turned, grabbing her hand and quickly pulling her to her feet. She wasn't expecting me to do this, so I took the opportunity and kissed her full on the mouth. After a second she relaxed against me and opened her mouth to my questing tongue. I kissed her good and hard for a full minute before pulling back.

"I had fun tonight. I really hope that you let me in, 'cause I really want to see you again soon. Don't get caught up in your own head," I said, staring into her eyes. She looked frightened, and I knew someone had really fucked her over in the past. "I'm going to go now so that you don't feel overwhelmed, but I'll text you tomorrow."

She followed me to the door and just as I was about to walk out I heard her say, "Wait."

I turned to look at her then.

"Thank you for tonight. I had a great time too," she said as she leaned in, and gave me a small, sweet kiss on the lips. I smiled, turned around, and left.

Chapter 11

Savannah

I sat on my couch after Charlie left, and reached for my wine. I didn't know what was wrong with me. I was supposed to be having casual sex, and my brain wouldn't shut off about it. I was starting to feel clingy toward him and I hated that. I didn't want a relationship. I just wanted to have hot, meaningless sex with a gorgeous, sweet, fun man, and instead my mind (and my uterus, for that matter) was yelling at me that he was the one, and to not let him walk out the door. I was on the verge of tears and I didn't know why. I was the one who distanced myself so he would leave, but now I felt abandoned. Even now, my body ached to be held by his big, strong arms, wanting comfort even from the source of my confusion.

I sat there, silently freaking out, for God knows how long. I felt like I was on the verge of an anxiety attack, which didn't surprise me considering I was so conflicted. It probably didn't help that I had that flashback of finding Greg today. That was never a good memory to relive before a first date. Or maybe it was, to remind myself that men were all cheating dirtbags who didn't deserve my trust. But Charlie wasn't like that. I didn't get even the smallest cheating vibe from him at all. *Fuck.* This was why I couldn't get my shit together.

As I drank my wine, I texted Lauren, desperately needing another woman's opinion to see if I was being as stupid as I felt I was.

Hey bitch.

Hey lady! I've been meaning to get a hold of you. How are you?

Well, that was a loaded question.

Having guy troubles...

Oh no! This calls for a ladies' night. Are you free tomorrow? Besides the fact that you are having problems, I am in desperate need of some girl time.

Sure! I'm off tomorrow so that will work perfectly. Mind if I invite my friend Anna? She loves having girls' nights and would be super pissed if I didn't invite her, I asked.

Of course! I need more girlfriends in my life.

Sweet! Wanna come over to my house? Or are we wanting to go out?

I hoped she wanted to come here. Call me lame, but I was never a big fan of going out. I hated driving downtown, it was always very loud, and without fail, there were constantly men who came to hit on a group of girls. I quickly texted Anna as I waited for Lauren to reply. Exactly thirty seconds later, the eccentric piercer texted me back with a message all in caps.

IT'S ABOUT TIME, BITCH! WHEN AND WHERE?!

Just then, Lauren texted me back that she would love to come over, and that she would bring the wine at seven. I texted Anna the time and location before I finished off my wine, and headed to bed.

True to his word, Charlie texted me the next day at noon to tell me that he couldn't stop thinking about me and that he hoped my day was going well. I wasn't quite sure how to respond, so I said a noncommittal "You too." I decided to take my mind off of things for the day, so I went grocery shopping for dinner that evening, cleaned my already clean apartment, baked some brownies, and finally at six, started cooking. I made my famous "white girl" enchiladas. They were not traditional or spicy in the least, but they were damn good. It was one of the only dishes that I was really good at making.

At exactly seven Anna busted in the door with an amused-looking Lauren on her heels.

"We're here, bitch!" she yelled. "Now where's the food and the wine opener? Let's get this party started!"

I had just taken the enchiladas out of the oven when they walked in. I had timed everything perfectly. Lauren walked over to me and gave me a big hug.

"Thanks for inviting me, girl! I'm so excited!" she exclaimed.

"Of course! I'm glad you could come," I replied. "How's the tattoo looking?"

"Oh, it's great! I think eventually it will need some touch-ups, but overall it healed really well." She pulled up the hem of her dress to show me how it was doing. I felt a surge of pride. I did that! It was so cool to think about sometimes. Anna walked in, and looked at Lauren's leg.

"Damn, are we showing skin already? I think I need some wine in me first. Or at least to be fed." She winked at us and we all laughed. "Shit, girl, you've got some nice legs!" Lauren blushed a little at her statement.

"Okay, okay. I just pulled the enchiladas out, so they still need a few minutes to cool. I will set the table, Lauren, you can pour us some wine, and Anna, why don't you get some music going up in here?" We all broke away to get everything ready, and soon we were all sitting at my small dining room table chowing down. Both girls exclaimed their appreciation for my food with almost every bite, and soon our plates were cleared. I bussed the table, and grabbed the wine bottle to refill all of our drinks.

"Okay, girl, spill," said Lauren.

I sighed. I knew this conversation was coming, and I was actually glad to have some female input, but I rarely talked about my feelings, and what was going on, so it was difficult for me.

"So, I basically slept with Charlie, wanting it to be a casual thing because of my fucked-up past, but now my stupid heart and womb are getting in the way and I'm developing feelings for him," I blurted out quickly. Both girls were silent and just looked at me for about five seconds. And then at the same time...

"You slept with Charlie? Wait, who's Charlie?" This came from Lauren.

"What fucked-up past?" This was from Anna.

"Lauren, Charlie is that gorgeous guy that saved me when we were at The Matador. He came into the shop to get a tattoo randomly, and then asked me on a date. Anna, my ex is a complete and utter tool." I left it at that, hoping that they wouldn't ask me any more about Greg. I wasn't going to say anything about him, it just sort of slipped out. No such luck...

"Savannah, that statement applies to most of the female population, so you need to elaborate."

"Fine. When I was back in Fort Collins a few years ago, I was having quite a bit of family problems. Believe it or not, I was completely different from how I am now. I was actually kind of preppy. I used to be a cheerleader back in high school, I got really good grades, was valedictorian, and was eventually going to go to Yale. You see, I never really wanted any of that, but my mother made me be involved in all of it. She said that as long as I was in her house, I had to wear the clothes that she bought for me, and I had to take part in all of the school activities that looked good on an application.

"Then some big family drama went down, and I decided to leave. The 'perfect' life and family that we were supposed to have was all a giant lie. I didn't want to be as fake as I was always taught, and to grow up to be as sheisty as my parents. So I decided to start working at a tattoo shop, apprenticing under a guy named Greg Williams. He was a great tattoo artist, and at first he was very nice and helpful. We began dating shortly after I started working there. Eventually, he became very critical of all my work. I realize now that he was probably a little jealous because I turned out to be a better artist than he was. I was establishing a very large clientele there, and the more clients I got, the harsher he was with my work.

"Looking back, I don't know why I stayed with him. Maybe because I was still seeking approval from the people in my life. It used to be my parents and family, and then when I left, it became Greg. Anyway, I stayed with him for much longer than I should've. I'd like to think that I would've left eventually on my own terms, but I'll never know. One night I came to surprise him at work with dinner and wine. When I arrived at the shop, I found him fucking one of his clients on his table. He didn't see me, so I went home and started packing my things and when he came home and I confronted him about it, he wasn't even sorry. He made it out to be my fault. Said that I never satisfied him sexually so of course he would go looking for something else. The only thing I never let him do in bed was the back door. He was always pretty rough whenever he would try. He wouldn't even ask me, he would just try to shove his way in. It never felt right with him. But yeah. That's what happened," I finished lamely, a little embarrassed that I went into so much detail. Talking about Greg so much was giving me a lot of unwanted flashbacks.

I was home one evening, which was typical for me. I was never a party girl. Greg still hadn't gotten back from work, which I thought was odd, considering he was supposed to be off an hour and a half earlier. Sometimes we ran a little late with clients, but never by this much. I had already tried calling him a half hour ago with no success.

I put a movie on to distract myself, trying not to worry or overreact, but I had a fairly overactive imagination so I tended to assume the worst. Maybe he had gotten into a car accident, *I thought.*

Just as I was about to leave and go look for him, he stumbled into the apartment, drunk off his ass.

"Greg, where have you been? I was worried," I said, rushing over to him to make sure that he didn't fall over.

"I was just out for a drink with the guys," he slurred.

"Well, why didn't you tell me you weren't coming home right away? And did you drive home like this? You can't even stand on your own," I scolded.

"Who are you? My mother? So what if I drove home? I'm fine," he spat, his breath reeking of whiskey. I also caught a whiff of perfume, but it was gone so quickly that I was sure I had imagined it.

"Greg, you could have killed yourself, or someone else! You should've called me. I would've come to pick you up."

Before I knew what was happening, he had me pushed up against the wall, his hand wrapping around my throat, not squeezing hard, but enough to scare the shit out of me. There was a look in his eyes that I had never seen before, like he had gone completely mad, and was no longer the man that I knew.

"Stop telling me what to do, bitch. I said I was fine," he growled in my face, and just like that, he let me go. Without giving me another glance, he stalked off toward the bedroom and slammed the door.

I slunk to the floor, clutching my neck as if I could erase what had just happened. Tears streamed down my face, and anxiety roiled in my stomach like a storm, making me feel like I was going to puke, but I didn't dare move from my spot on the carpet.

It was just the alcohol, I told myself. That was all it was. He would never have done it otherwise. I kept saying that to myself over and over, repeating it like a mantra.

I fell asleep in that same spot, hours later.

"Savannah," Lauren said, breaking me out of my daydream, "I'm so sorry that Greg was such an asshole, but not all guys are like that. You just have to find the right one. And from the sounds of it, Charlie is a very good guy. Not to mention how he saved you from that asshole at dinner, and he still asked you on a date after you wouldn't give him the time of day."

I thought about that, and I knew she was right.

"I know he's probably a great guy, but I just have such a hard time trusting people. After all the shit with my family and then with Greg, I'm just kind of a loner now. It's not easy for me to trust anyone, especially men. Anna, you've known me for how long now and I've never even hung out with you outside of work. It's not because I don't think you're awesome, or that I don't want to hang out with you, I just have trouble putting myself out there and opening myself up to people again."

"Well, maybe you can start with us, lady. We both love you, and we won't hurt you. Plus, it seems like you already are. Texting us to come here and talk to you about all of this is a big step," Anna said seriously, surprising me. She was right of course, but it caught me off guard because she wasn't acting like her normally loud, joking self.

"Okay, so what should I do about Charlie then?" I asked, still confused and unsure. This conversation had turned more into a discussion about my past than what I should do.

"Dude, just go for it. You've got nothing to lose." This came from Lauren.

I took a deep breath and made a decision. She was right. I couldn't hide away from everybody forever.

"Will you both help me decide what to text him?" I asked nervously.

"Fuck yeah, bitch! Let's send that sexy ass motherfucker a hot picture of you."

"Ooooh that's a great idea!" said Lauren.

We eventually decided to send a selfie of me on my bed, wearing my sexy black lace baby doll, a candle lit in the background, with a text that said *Wish you were here.*

Chapter 12

Charlie

I looked at the picture of Savannah at least a dozen times over the next few hours. It was finally a slow night at work, and this was good in that I finally got a little bit of a break, but bad in the sense that all I could concentrate on was Savannah.

I immediately texted her back to say *You're killin' me, babe,* and she replied with a winky face. I was really tempted to go over to her place after work, but I wouldn't be off until late. Or early, depending on how you looked at it. It took everything in me to give her a little space after the other night. I could tell that she needed some time to adjust to everything. Most of the time with women, I took my time before I decided if I wanted to be with them or not (most of the time the answer was not), but with Savannah, I didn't have that feeling. I wanted to make her mine right away. It made me jealous thinking of the guys who would come into the shop to have her tattoo them, her gentle, soft hands on them when she brought a tattoo gun to their skin.

Fuck. Maybe I should call her, I thought. It rang three times before she answered.

"Hello, sexy," she said in a sultry voice. I couldn't stop the groan that escaped.

"Hey, beautiful. I haven't been able to concentrate all night due to the sexy ass picture you sent me. It's taking everything in me not to go over to your house and rip that nightie off of you."

"Well, I wouldn't object to that," she said with a giggle.

"Tell him to send us a picture of his sexy ass!" some girl shouted in the background. I laughed.

"Who was that?"

"That was my friend Anna. You met her when you came into the shop. She's the hot blonde with lots of piercings and no filter. I decided that I needed a girls' night. My friend Lauren is here too. You met her too, actually. She was at The Matador that night we met. She has the silver-purple hair and a nose ring."

"Yeah, I remember both of them. Why did you feel like you needed a girls' night?" I asked. I had a feeling it had something to do with the fact that we slept together.

"Well...I guess I was just feeling a little confused about the stuff that happened between us, and I just needed the opinion of someone who was less fucked up than I was." Bingo. Called it.

"Baby, you aren't screwed up. You've just had some screwed-up things happen to you."

There was a long pause. Then… "How do you know I've had screwed-up things happen to me?"

"I can just tell, Savannah. Now, did you decide to send me that sexy picture or was it the girls?"

She busted out laughing.

"Mostly me. I just needed a little encouragement."

"Well, tell those lovely ladies that I appreciate all the encouragement, and to keep it up." I could hear her relaying my message to them, followed by lots of yelling and laughing.

"As long as you send us a picture of your sexy ass tonight, hot stuff!"

I heard Anna yell in the background.

"Tell Anna that she couldn't handle my sexy ass," I said, hearing yells of protest as Savannah told her what I said. "Well, have fun with your girls' night, gorgeous. I'll talk to you soon."

"Okay. Talk to you soon," she said and she hung up. I couldn't tell if I was being hopeful and she sounded disappointed or not.

After I hung up, Bill, another co-worker, leaned over with a surprised look on his face. "You're chasing after a girl? You never do that."

"I know," I said. "This one is something special though. At first I thought that maybe it was the chase? Now I know that it's not that."

"Did something happen between you two?"

"We've gone on a couple of dates. I can tell that she likes me, but something in her past is making her very skittish." I exhaled loudly, frustrated. "I don't know, Bill. I've never been in this situation before. I don't really know what to do. I know that I need to tread carefully, but I know that she needs to be pushed too. I don't want to fuck this up."

"Well, it sounds like you've been doing good so far. She's still talking to you and sending you pictures, which are good signs. I'm sure whatever comes up, you'll know what to do."

"Thanks, Bill. I hope you're right," I said, standing, and heading to the bathroom.

After I closed the door, I grabbed my phone and turned on my camera. Facing away from the mirror, I reached my phone around, pulled up my shirt a little so some of my back was showing, and took a picture of my backside for the girls, thinking that it would make them laugh. I sent the picture with a wink to Savannah.

As soon as I stepped out of the bathroom, the alarm went off. I put my phone away and got to work.

I hadn't checked my phone until I got home at the end of the night. As soon as I walked in, I tossed my keys down, and pulled my phone out to see that I had five texts from Savannah.

I like talking to you. I think we should do it more often.

HOT DAAAAYYYMN! But it was supposed to be OUT of the jeans.

Sorry, that last one was from Anna...she has a point though.

I can't stop thinking about that sexy ass pounding into me from behind while you spank me.

So I'm officially drunk. Sorry about all the drunk texts. Good night. Text me tomorrow...please.

Fuck. I was hard from that fourth text. And very happy that she liked talking to me. And damn did I love the sound of her begging. I looked over at the clock and read 3:14. Well, shit. I decided to send her one more text before bed. At least then I would hopefully wake up to another one from her. I typed out a quick response before debating what to do next.

One of the downsides of this job was the fucked-up hours. I was still wide awake from my shift. And hungry. I popped open a beer and made myself a quesadilla. Not the healthiest option, but I didn't feel like putting in the effort for anything more time-consuming. Plus, I made a bomb ass quesadilla.

Ten minutes later, I was sitting in front of the TV browsing through Netflix. I didn't watch too much TV, but one of the guys was telling me that *Stranger Things* was really good. Ah, fuck it. I turned it on and settled in with my dinner.

Three hours later and five beers down, I looked at the clock—6:30—and realized that I had become addicted. This show was so interesting. Not to mention the fact that I couldn't figure out what the fuck was going on. I had my suspicions, but I didn't know for sure. And I had a feeling that I wouldn't know for a few more episodes.

Savannah still hadn't responded to my text yet, but it was still early and she had been drinking the night before, so she probably wasn't up yet. As I lay on the couch, dozing off, I imagined what it would be like to be next to her in bed, spooning her from behind and stroking her hair. I didn't realize until Savannah came along how lonely I was. My body ached to be next to her, hold her, and seek comfort in her embrace. I just hoped that I would get to experience that eventually.

Then I smiled to myself, remembering the night before. Her sober self wasn't ready to admit what we had yet, but her drunk self was. It was only a matter of time, and I was patient...

Chapter 13

Savannah

I woke with a massive headache and the feeling that I might hurl. Damn, I drank a lot last night. I went into the living room, and found Anna and Lauren sprawled out on the couch. Anna woke as I came closer.

"I had a sexy dream about your man's hot ass last night," she said and winked at me. It didn't have the effect she was probably hoping for since her hair was a huge ratty mess, her makeup was smeared, and she had wine stains on her lips.

"Did you look like you do now in your dream? 'Cause I can see why Charlie couldn't resist you," I joked as I started cleaning a bit. "Are you guys hungry? We could go to brunch. Kill our hangovers with some mimosas and Bloodys."

"Oh God, that sounds delicious," Lauren said as she stretched out, putting her foot in Anna's face in the process.

"Okay, great. Why don't we all get ready and then we can go to Snooze?" Snooze was the best breakfast place in Denver.

I took a quick shower, wrapped up in a towel, and went to my room after yelling at the girls that the bathroom was free. I unwrapped the towel from my body, put it around my hair, and went to my nightstand to grab my phone. I saw that I had a text from Charlie at 3:15 in the morning, and everything from last night came rushing back to me. I opened our message thread and turned red from embarrassment. At least drunk Savannah was good at dirty talking.

Damn, baby. I like the sound of you begging me. Maybe next time we get together I'll make you beg me to pound you from behind like your text said. And you can see my ass anytime you want... Good night, sexy.

I locked my phone with a huge smile on my face while I debated what to wear. I decided on a pair of tan jeans and a black strappy tank top. I put my hair up and finished the look with a cream-colored bandana headband. I played some music as I did my makeup and then put my glasses on. I didn't feel like wearing my contacts. When I was finished getting ready, I went out to the living room to wait for the girls.

My music was interrupted as my phone started ringing. *Mom. Fuck.* I hated talking to my mother. I ignored it, not wanting to get into whatever it was that she wanted. That was the only reason she ever called me. I wondered what it was this time. A minute later, a voice mail icon popped up.

"Savannah darling, it's your mother. Why aren't you answering? Isn't it your day off? You better not still be in bed. Well, I was just calling to see how you were doing. I also wanted to talk to you about something, so call me back when you get this."

God, she was so full of shit. And I knew she wanted something. Oh well. It's not like I was going to call her back. Just then the girls came out.

"Are you ready, bitch? I'm starving." This came from Anna, of course.

"Damn straight. I'll drive," I said.

After waiting half an hour at Snooze, we were seated. Lauren ordered an extra-spicy Bloody Mary, and Anna and I ordered peach mimosas. We all then ordered French toast with eggs and hash browns. Nobody was dieting today. My phone started ringing. I rolled my eyes as I saw it was my mother again. I hit ignore as I took a long drink of my mimosa. The girls exchanged a look and then the questions started.

"Who was that?" Lauren asked. "And why do you look like you want to punch someone right now?"

"It was just my mom. She called me this morning too."

"Well, that still doesn't answer my question as to why you want to punch someone."

I huffed as a response and took a longer drink, draining it. I reached for the carafe and poured another.

"Well, I think we have quite a story here, don't you, Lauren?" asked Anna with a sly look on her face.

"It is quite a story. You guys are just finding out all sorts of shit about me, aren't you?" I said, pretty bitterly, I might add. "Sorry, I'm not trying to sound like a bitch, but my mother gets on my last nerve. She only calls me when she needs something. Remember when I told you that I used to be a cheerleader and all that shit? It was all because of her. She always pushed that kind of stuff on me. She was grooming me to marry the perfect man. It was always about how to be the perfect daughter, and eventually how to be the perfect wife, never about what I wanted or what I thought was best. She used to have all of these housewife types of friends that she always wanted to impress. I think that was one of the reasons that she was like that. She has always been into appearances, and she of course had to be the perfect wife. That was the only true purpose for a woman, she said, to be a good reflection on your husband. I let her manipulate me for a long time because I wanted her approval and the love of my father. It didn't end up mattering in the end anyway. I never ended up getting his love or her approval. After I found out the truth about him, I got the hell outta Dodge."

The girls were both captivated, but I hadn't even scratched the surface of all of the fucked-up shit that happened in my family. Probably all of it being the reason why I was with Greg so long and why I let him control me. All because of the fucked-up ideals my mother instilled in me about marriage and a woman's role in life. I could still hear her voice in my head whenever I went to do something "unladylike." *Savannah, you have to always be on your best behavior. You never know who will be watching. You reflect on your husband, and will be on his arm like a trophy.* Shit like that. No wonder I've always rebelled when people try to tell me I can't do something.

"So are you going to tell us what the truth is about him? Or do we have to guess?" asked Lauren.

"Ooh, my money is on a secret, dirty affair gone wrong!" Anna exclaimed. I wished it was as simple as an affair.

"No, it wasn't that. At least not that I know of. Knowing my father, he probably had one going on too, but no. My father was a politician. His campaign was fairly successful at first, but then it started slowing down. Somehow, he still had lots of money to run it and keep him going. I found out later that he was selling drugs on the side to pay for his campaign to run for the House of Representatives.

"After he was convicted, I got the hell out, much to my mother's dismay. She's still at his side, trying to make it seem like everything was pinned on him. He's in jail to this day and it's been almost five years. I think he actually is supposed to be released soon, and that's probably why she's calling me. I'll bet you anything that she wants me to be there by their side to show 'family unity.' Fuck that. Fuck them." After my rant I realized that I had a few angry tears streaking down my face. I batted them away and drained my full mimosa in one gulp.

"Jesus. How long was he doing it for?" Lauren asked.

"Years. Three, I think?"

"What kind of drugs, Savannah?" Anna inquired.

"Heroin. You can't get much worse than that. Except for maybe meth, but still."

"Well, shit." Anna again, of course. "No wonder you don't want to talk to that bitch of a mother. I wouldn't either."

"Yeah, I'm so sorry, Savannah. I'm glad you told us though," said Lauren. "Have you talked to anyone other than us about it?"

"Well, everyone back home knows my family, so of course they've all heard about what had happened. My so-called 'friends' never talked to me after that, not wanting to be seen with the drug dealer's daughter. After I left, I changed my number, not wanting any attention on the matter, especially from the media. I haven't talked to any of my friends from high school since. I gave my mother my new number, but I now realize that was a huge mistake. I guess I still want contact with her even though she is a bitch. Whatever."

"Fuck. I totally remember this. It was on the news and everything. I also remember your mom vehemently claiming that he didn't do it!" Anna exclaimed.

"Yeah, that's her. She's a piece of work. She knows he did it, no matter what bullshit she spouts."

"Wellll, it sounds like it's time for a subject change. Did your sexy man text you back after all of your drunk sexting last night?" Anna asked.

"Oh God," I said, turning bright red. "First of all, he's not my man, he's just a sexy man. Second of all, I plead the Fifth."

"Oh, he totally did. What did he say? You have to tell us. We're the ones who helped you come up with what to write," Lauren said.

I rolled my eyes while I unlocked my phone and handed it over to them so I didn't have to say it out loud.

"Dayymn, girl! When did you write the one about him smacking your ass? You're dirtier than I thought," Anna said as I blushed profusely.

"Well, believe it or not, I do know my way around a bedroom. I just don't broadcast it like you do, Anna."

"Hey! You know you love hearing about all my sexcapades. And besides, I don't tell you all about the super dirty stuff."

"Oh really? Wasn't it just last week when you were telling me all about that guy that had fingers in your puss and ass and it made you squirt all over him?"

"Anna, you can squirt? I thought that was an urban legend," Lauren said.

"Well, shit, Savannah, if I had known you were going to bring that up, I would've had another couple mimosas down by now," Anna said. "And it's no urban legend, honey, but it is phenomenal."

Just then our server came over with our food. We ate in silence since we were all ravenous from drinking so much the night before. When we finished eating I realized that all of last night was pretty much spent talking about me and my stupid man problems.

"Lauren, how are things going with you? Have you found a job yet?" I asked.

"You know, I did. I'm still doing hair, unfortunately, but I couldn't keep not working. I was going crazy. So for now I'm at Floyd's Barbershop over on Champa."

"Well, that's good! How do you like it?"

"It's fine. It pays the bills for now. It's usually very busy 'cause it's right downtown, which is good, but I am so fucking exhausted. Like all the time."

"Yeah, we know how that goes. We're pretty consistently busy too. Right, Anna?" I asked.

"Yeah, for sure. At the end of my shift, sometimes I feel like piercing my own eyeballs just so I have an excuse not to come in the next day."

"Well, enough about work. How are you and Ryan?" I asked.

"Ooh who's Ryan? He sounds hot." Anna, naturally.

Lauren chuckled and said, "Ryan is my boyfriend. He's why I moved here. We've been together for almost three years now, and we are doing great. Our anniversary is next month and Ryan says he's planning something but he won't tell me what."

"Oh shit, girl. You's gettin' a ring!" Anna exclaimed.

"Yeah, babe. I bet you any money you'll be engaged by the time your anniversary is over," I said, smiling.

"Yeah, I have a feeling too," Lauren said, "but I'm trying not to get my hopes up just in case it doesn't happen."

"Yeah, good plan. Even though you know it's going to happen anyway," I said.

Lauren blushed a little and smiled profusely. "Well, either way I'll be happy. So Anna, are you with anyone?"

"Oh shit, no. Who do you know that would put up with my crazy ass? I'm loud, I have no fucking filter, and I have the mouth of a sailor. I've dated a few guys but they all fled pretty quickly. Just one-night stands for me," Anna said, trying to sound nonchalant, but for the first time, maybe ever, I saw a vulnerability in her.

"Anna, you are definitely crazy, but it's one of your great qualities. That's why we love you so much. Those other guys just weren't right for you. Don't worry. You will find someone who loves how fun and outgoing you are. Maybe even someone who's as crazy as you," I said.

"Oh, God. Can you imagine? I think we would get arrested or some shit like that within the first day," Anna said, laughing.

"It will be all over the news about how the two of you had sex in public and I will have to bail your ass out of jail."

We continued chatting and drinking at Snooze for the next hour before I drove all of us back to my apartment. The girls said goodbye to me and we hugged, promising to have another girls' night soon.

I headed back into my apartment and immediately collapsed onto the couch for a quick nap.

Sometime later I woke to my phone ringing. Not even glancing at it, I answered groggily.

"Savannah! Are you sleeping?! It's two in the afternoon!" I was immediately awake, hearing my mother scolding me over the phone. "Have you been sleeping all morning? You haven't answered any of my calls."

"Hello, Mother. And no, I was just taking a nap. I went to breakfast with a few girlfriends this morning," I replied.

"Well, you know how I don't like it when you don't answer my phone calls. It's not respectful, dear," she continued, droning on while I rolled my eyes. "But anyway, darling, I'm calling because your father is finally being released next week and I need you there to show your support. Now, I haven't seen you for a while, but I'm assuming you'll need to be groomed a little bit before then, so I was thinking we could go have a girls' day at the salon. We could get our hair highlighted and our nails done. What day works for you?"

Jesus. Only my mother could talk that long without taking a single breath. And I fucking called it. I knew that the only reason she was calling me was because of that bastard.

"Mom, I'm not doing any of that" was all I said to her.

"Savannah!" she exclaimed. "Don't talk like that. You are coming and that's that. Now tell me what day you are free so we can go to the salon."

"Mother. I'm. Not. Going. I'm sorry, but I'm not. I'll talk to you later," I said as I hung up. I turned my phone off and tossed it on the table before lying back down and falling asleep for the rest of the afternoon.

Chapter 14

Charlie

It had been three days since I last talked to Savannah, and I was going a little crazy. I was trying to give her space, but I didn't know how much longer I could stand it. I finally had a day off, so I decided to do something nice to show her I was thinking about her. I had already gotten her flowers for our first date, so I debated what else I could get her. All women loved chocolates, right? I looked up food baskets online and found a ton of stuff. Well, I had already decided on chocolates, so I narrowed it down to a few sweet options. The one I eventually picked was by Ghirardelli, and had a million different types of chocolate in it, along with caramel corn, cookies, and a ton of other sweet shit that I didn't even recognize. I added it to my cart and included a simple message.

Thinking of you, beautiful. Charlie.

I sent it to her work, hoping that it would arrive the same day. While I waited, I decided to go for a hike. It had been a while since I went on one, so I changed, put on some sunscreen, and packed a lunch, figuring that I would eat on the hike when I was ready for a break. My favorite place to go was Chautauqua Park in Boulder. It was beautiful there, and the mountain was steep enough to give me a pretty good workout. It was about a thirty to forty minute drive to get there, so I rolled my windows down and put on some Rage Against the Machine.

It wasn't too packed when I got there, considering it was a Tuesday morning. As I started out, I thought for maybe the fiftieth time that I wished I had a dog. It was just so hard with the weird hours I worked, and the fact that I was sometimes gone for more than twelve hours in a day. We always had dogs growing up, so it was a strange and new feeling for me not to come home to anyone or anything at the end of my day. It was kind of depressing actually. Oh well. Maybe if things went well with Savannah, we could get one together when we moved in together.

Shit. Where did that thought come from? I knew I liked her, but we were nowhere close to those thoughts yet. Plus she already had a cat. Maybe she didn't even like dogs. But who didn't like dogs? Jesus. I was rambling even in my own thoughts.

I really needed to quiet my mind and enjoy everything around me. I stopped for a second, closed my eyes, and focused on my breathing. Quickly, I was able to focus on the feeling of the sunshine on my face and the smell of the mountain air. I opened my eyes, smiling, and started back up the mountain.

By the time I reached the top of the trail, I was drenched in sweat and starving. I found a nice little rock to eat on and have my lunch. Fuck, a beer sounded so good. Maybe I would have to stop by Old Chicago on my way back and have one. Just as I was finishing off my sandwich, my phone dinged with a text. I opened it and smiled as I saw that it was from Savannah.

Thanks for the basket. It's delicious.

Hmm. That didn't sound like Savannah. I wondered if something was up. I didn't think it had anything to do with me. She seemed pretty content and playful in our last messages. I decided to call her to see if something really was up. She answered on the fourth ring.

"Hello."

"Hey, beautiful. It's Charlie. I'm glad you're enjoying my basket."

"Oh, hey. Yes I am. Thank you for sending it."

"I wanted to let you know I've been thinking of you. I know you're a little skittish, if you will, about the whole relationship thing, but I promise I won't bite. Not unless you want me to of course," I said, deliberately putting a teasing tone in my voice.

"I like it when you bite," she replied, chuckling.

"I know you do. You ask me to do it harder." She laughed even more at that. "But more importantly, I just wanted to call to see if you were okay. You haven't contacted me in a few days, and you seemed a little off in your text."

"Well, thanks for checking in. I'm okay. I just have a lot of family shit going down right now, and my head hasn't quite been right," she said, sighing deeply. "I've been meaning to reach out to you, but I haven't had the capacity to even think about anything else right now."

"I'm so sorry, Savannah. You don't need to explain, but if you ever need to talk to anyone, just know that I'm here for you. Take all the time you need to get everything sorted out. I'll be here when you're ready."

"Thanks, Charlie. I'll tell you eventually, but it's too fresh for me to talk about right now. I really do love the food basket you sent. I've already eaten half of it, and Anna is eyeing the other half as we speak. It definitely cheered me up when the chick that came in with a basket of sweet goodies told me she had a delivery for me," she said with a smile in her voice. Then I heard a slap and her yelling at someone in the background. "Hey, bitch! I told you I wasn't sharing!" she shouted, laughing. I guess Anna tried to swipe something while she was preoccupied.

"Well, good, beautiful. That's all I wanted. But I'll let you get back to work, or to eating more sweets. I just wanted to call and check on you. The ball is in your court, so call or text me when you're ready. Have a good day, baby."

"Thanks, Charlie. I'll text you soon. Bye, handsome."

I smiled as I hung up. I was glad I was able to cheer her up, even if it was only just for a little bit. I finished off my lunch and headed back down the mountain. By the time I got to my car, it was around four and I was craving a beer so effing bad. I drove to the Old Chicago in Broomfield and took a seat at the bar. I ordered a Fat Tire and realized that I was hungry again. When the server brought my beer, I also ordered some pepperoni rolls and a side salad. As I nursed my drink and waited for my food, I looked around at the billion TVs and saw a news channel doing a story on Paul Ajax. Why did that last name sound familiar? I asked the bartender to turn the volume up on that station. As soon as she did, Paul and his wife came on screen, doing a live interview. Paul, however, didn't say a word the entire interview. His wife did all of the talking for him while he stood there looking like an arrogant ass.

"We are so pleased that Paul has been released. I'm sure all of you know that he got out early due to good behavior. We are, however, disappointed in the justice system. Paul never committed the crimes that he did time for. He should never have had to serve his sentence, and now that he has been released, we are going to do everything we can to find out who framed him." The wife basically said the whole thing without taking a breath. Quite a statement considering that all of the evidence pointed directly to him. Poor lady. Someone had a big case of denial. "I would like to thank all of our friends who have been so supportive during this time. We sincerely appreciate the money and effort that you have put in to helping us solve who is really behind these crimes. Our daughter, Savannah, couldn't be here today due to illness, but I know she would love to thank all of you as well. She supports her father just as much as I do, and is thrilled he is out." She continued to drone on and on, but I didn't hear any of it. Savannah Ajax. That's where I knew that last name.

I knew for a fact that Savannah wasn't sick, so I felt like her mother just said all of that shit about her because she wanted it to look like their family was united. What a bitch. Now I knew why Savannah had been distant. Damn. I wanted to go check on her but I didn't know if she wanted that. Or for me to know what was going on with her family. I know I wouldn't want anyone knowing that. Fuck it. I was going to risk visiting her after she got home from work. I couldn't wait after hearing this news.

Chapter 15

Savannah

Lana Del Rey sang about her pussy tasting like Pepsi Cola as I soaked in the bath. Fuck this day. Fuck my family. Fuck my mother. I couldn't believe she said all that shit about me on national fucking television. Actually I could totally believe it, but still. *No, don't think about it, Savannah,* I scolded myself. I was taking a bath and not thinking about my shit day. I pulled out all the stops too. I had a mud mask, a bath bomb, and lavender-scented bubble bath, candles, music, and lots and lots of wine. I was utterly determined to forget my day. Except the part where Charlie sent me the most delicious chocolate basket I've ever had the pleasure of eating. Damn, I salivated just thinking about it, and I smiled in spite of myself thinking about Charlie.

He'd been so great this last week. I don't know how he knew I needed space, but he did. I had finally felt like my thoughts concerning him were composed, and I was comfortable with my feelings toward him. He was nothing like Greg. He couldn't be further from Greg actually. Even at the beginning of our relationship, I had never felt like this with him.

Damn, I looked down and realized that I'd finished off the rest of my wine. I got out to go get some more when I heard a knock on the door. That was strange. It was like eight at night. I took a detour to my room to grab a robe, and put it on as I made my way to the front door. As I opened the door I caught a quick glimpse of Charlie before he barged in to give me a big hug. After I got over the surprise, I sunk into the embrace. God he smelled delicious.

He pulled back to inspect me and asked, "Are you all right?"

"Charlie, I'm fine. What's the big deal?"

"I...saw the news earlier."

Fuck. Of course he did. At least with him being here, I knew he wasn't repulsed by me after seeing my shit-head parents on TV.

"Oh, great. Yeah, that's my ridiculous family. I try not to have anything to do with them, but my mother has been up my ass with all the stuff going on with my dad. I haven't seen or talked to him since he got arrested."

"I'm so sorry, baby. I wanted to come and check on you to see how you were. I know you probably don't want to talk about it, but if you ever do, I'm here. And if you don't, that's totally okay with me too. I don't need to know the details unless you want to share them with me."

"Thanks. Maybe eventually I'll tell you the whole story, but I'm really tired of thinking and talking about it." I smiled at him.

"Okay, babe, whatever you need." He smiled back at me before his brow furrowed as he took in my appearance. "Why do you have black shit all over your face?"

I chuckled as I said, "I was taking a bath and this is a mud mask. It's been a long day and I needed to unwind."

"Oh, I see. Well, do you want me to leave?"

"No, but I would like to finish my bath. Do you want to sit in the bathroom with me?"

"What kind of question is that? I get to sit in your bathroom while you're naked and wet for my viewing pleasure?" he asked.

"Okay, well, let me just refill my wine first," I said, laughing.

"No, I'll get it for you. Just go back to your bath, and I'll be there in just a second."

Oh God. I think I may have swooned. A gorgeous man bringing me wine and taking care of me while I took a bath? Yes please. A minute later, he came in bearing much more than just wine. He handed me the glass and then a piece of chocolate as he sat down, holding more goodies from my basket. I moaned as the chocolate hit my tongue, and then I washed it down with some wine, and moaned again as it changed the flavor of the chocolate. I opened my eyes, and looked at Charlie just as his eyes darkened.

"God, I love that sound. I wish I could've been there to witness when you first got this basket. I bet you would've made that sound over and over," he said, instantly making me wet.

"I may have," I said evasively. "If you hand me more of those goodies though, I'm sure I can reenact how I responded to receiving the basket."

He walked over to the tub, and fed me a chocolate-covered strawberry. I wrapped my lips around it and sucked a bit before biting down. I licked my lips free of juice before chewing, my eyes on him the whole time. After I swallowed, he held more strawberry out for me. I took another bite and then I grabbed his finger, bringing it to my lips. His breathing became shallow as I sucked his finger into my mouth and groaned, scraping my teeth lightly along his finger. His finger popped free from my suction and I swallowed the rest of the fruit.

"Mmm. Delicious," I said, licking my lips again. I heard him growl as he took a bite of strawberry for himself before leaning down to kiss me. The juice from the strawberry leaked into my mouth and coated my tongue as he pushed his own tongue between my lips. I bit his lip, as a ferocity like I'd never felt clawed through my veins. I ripped at his hair trying to pull him into the tub with me. He chuckled before slowly breaking the kiss and pulling back.

"Easy, baby. I know you're feeling overwhelmed by everything going on, but I'm right here, and I'm not going anywhere. Maybe you should get out of the bath and we can go to bed?" God, he sounded so unaffected. I didn't know how he managed to sound that way when I could clearly see the evidence of his arousal pointing at me through his pants.

"Yeah, okay. Let me just wash this mask off of my face," I said. When I finished, he grabbed my hands and hoisted me out of the tub before drying me off. As soon as I was mostly dry, he picked me up and carried me to my room before throwing me on the bed.

Holy. Shit.

I had never had anyone treat me like a china doll and a dirty whore all at the same time. And. I. Loved. It.

He crawled over me slowly, his eyes dragging over every inch of me. His lips latched on to mine again, and he took his time making love to my mouth. His tongue coaxed my lips open as he swallowed my groans of pleasure. I was quick to become impatient, wanting him inside me, wanting to feel the connection between us now that I had accepted it, but Charlie had other plans. He took his time with me, and as much as that frustrated me, it made me a million times wetter, and I fell a little bit harder for him.

His tongue swirled in my mouth as his hands explored my naked body. They started at my breasts, tweaking my nipples with his fingers, my piercings making them much more sensitive. With my hands wrapped around his low back, I pulled him on top of me and moved my pussy along the erection straining through his jeans. He groaned as he pushed his hips into mine. For about a minute, he couldn't seem to control himself as he thrust against me, soaking up pleasure just as I did before he broke away and started moving down my body. His lips wrapped around my piercing, and sucked my tight nipple into his hot mouth. His fingers brushed against my clit and I went crazy. I started writhing on the bed, even though I hadn't come yet. He swirled round and round, while his mouth sucked harder on my nipple, and his other hand played with my other breast.

I became so undone that I couldn't help moving my hips in rhythm with his motions and latching my fingers into his hair, pulling his mouth as close as I could. Pretty soon I felt myself building, climbing higher and higher. He caught on to the fact that I was about to come and switched up his pattern, increasing and prolonging my pleasure. He plunged his fingers inside of me and grazed my clit with his thumb as he pumped his fingers in and out. Within seconds I exploded around his fingers, my pussy pulsing and flooding with release. He smiled arrogantly as he removed his fingers from my body and inserted them into his mouth, cleaning them of my wetness.

"Okay, baby, you've got me good, ready, and wet. Will you please fuck me now?" I asked as I started undressing him.

He laughed as he stood up to remove his pants. As I lay there admiring the view, I drifted my hand lower, unable to help myself. He was so sexy that I had to touch myself as I drank in his beautiful body. His eyes blazed as they latched on to the movement of my hand. His own hand wandered down to his hard cock, pumping it a few times before he crawled back onto the bed with me. I looked down to see a drop of liquid coming out of the tip of his dick, and my mouth watered at the thought of tasting him. As much as I wanted to, I didn't have the patience, and I didn't think he did either, for that matter. So instead, I swiped my thumb along the top, gathering his precum on my digit before inserting it into my mouth and sucking. That was the last straw for him as he knocked my hand out of the way and latched his mouth on to mine before dragging his erection through my wet folds, my previous release coating his cock.

I moaned as his head hit my clit over and over. Just as I was about to come again, he stopped and positioned himself at my entrance. I opened my eyes and looked into his green depths before he slowly entered me, torturing both of us. Once he was fully inside of me, he held himself still for a few seconds.

"I'm sorry, gorgeous. I just need a second to get a hold of myself. Otherwise this will be over much too soon," he said, his body trembling slightly. My pussy clenched around him at the need in his voice. He groaned again. "God, Savannah. You're killing me here." I chuckled and gave him the minute he needed.

Before long, he started moving. Slowly at first, and then picking up speed. The top of his groin rubbed against my clit with every thrust, and I could feel my orgasm building once again. I hiked my legs higher up his body and squeezed him with every movement, my hands moving to his ass to encourage him deeper inside my body. The closer I got to finishing, the more manic I became. Charlie, sensing that I was close, flipped us over so I was on top.

"Fuck me. Ride me, Savannah. Use my body for your pleasure," he said, lying there so I could do whatever I wanted to him. Letting go of my nerves of being in charge, I started moving. The longer I moved, the more animalistic I became. I got really into it, spiraling my hips and leaning far back. Charlie reached up and grabbed my tits, helping me move, and stimulating me even more.

"Fuck, Charlie, I'm close."

"Yeah, baby. I want to feel you coming all over my cock."

His dirty words and unforgiving hands sent me over the edge as I ground myself against him, crying out loudly and incoherently. My release seemed to last forever as Charlie groaned and said, "Oh shit, beautiful, you're leaking all over me. I can feel your greedy cunt milking my dick over and over. Oh, fuck, I'm coming." He pumped into me from below before I felt his hot release coating my insides.

We lay there, panting for breath for a minute, before I gave him a quick kiss and slowly removed my body from on top of his. I winced as

I felt him slide out of me, along with a good amount of semen. I made my way into the bathroom, awkwardly trying to keep my legs closed as much as possible to prevent more from getting all over my floor. Charlie came into the bathroom right as I was wiping myself. I grabbed a baby wipe, and handed it to him to clean himself off. This time felt different. I didn't want him to leave like I did last time. I didn't feel that horrible conflict and indecision. All I felt was a deep contentment. I looked at his face and could see he felt the same way I did.

"Can I stay the night, baby? I don't want to leave you," he asked, echoing my thoughts.

"Yes. I don't want you to leave me," I finally admitted out loud. There would be no turning back now.

Chapter 16

Charlie

I crawled into bed next to Savannah and pulled her tight against me, my front to her back. She moaned as she curled in closer, rubbing her ass against my crotch. I struggled not to get turned on again. As much as I could've gone for another round, I was just happy to lie here and hold her. I loved being able to be her comfort and support. I was really starting to fall hard for her.

She had been different tonight. Not afraid of our connection. It seemed like she wanted to tap into it more, which meant that all bets were off. I couldn't stand giving her space the week before, but I did it because I knew she needed it. I didn't think I could do it again.

As I lay there, Jorge decided to come up and join the party, and he cuddled up right next to Savannah. It was like we were three spoons. Before long, Savannah's breathing started to deepen and Jorge added to the noise by purring. My last thought before I drifted off was that I could fall asleep like this every night...

I woke to a kitty paw in my face. Jorge stared down at me as if to ask why I was still sleeping. I stretched and looked next to me, seeing Savannah sprawled out on her stomach hugging a pillow. I slowly got out of bed so as not to disturb her. Jorge followed me before veering off toward his food dish. I made a quick trip to the bathroom before going out to feed Jorge. As soon as he was satisfied that I had put enough food in his dish, he started chowing down.

The clock on the stove read 9:03. Perfect. Savannah and I both had the day off and I planned to spend the whole day with her. Starting with breakfast. I broke out my headphones and started some jams as I rummaged through her fridge. I wasn't an excellent cook, but I could handle the basics. Deciding on scrambled eggs and bacon, I got to work.

Twenty minutes later, I had loaded up everything onto a tray (including two Bloody Marys) and went back into the bedroom. Just as I closed the door behind me, Savannah started to stir. She yawned and sat up just as I set the tray on the bed. She stared at it for about ten seconds before looking up at me, slightly teary.

"You made all this for me?" she asked, a slight hitch in her voice.

"Of course I did, baby. Hasn't anyone ever made you breakfast in bed before?"

"No. I've never had anyone do anything like this for me. Even my mom never cooked for us. We had a cook at home, but it was her job. Thank you so much. This looks delicious," she said as she took a drink of her Bloody, and started in on the food.

I smiled as I followed her lead, while silently reeling on the inside. No wonder she kept me at arm's length earlier. No one had ever shown her true affection before.

"So, I know we both have the day off. I was thinking we should have a day together. Besides the few dates we've been on, we haven't spent that much time together," I said.

"I would love that. What did you have in mind?"

"Well, there's a carnival in town. Is that something you might be interested in?" I asked.

"That sounds great. I haven't been to a carnival in years!"

After we both finished eating and getting dressed, we still had a few hours to kill before the carnival, so we decided to go shopping in the Highlands. We walked around the neighborhoods hand in hand, window-shopping at a few places, until we came across a lingerie shop.

"Wanna go in?" I asked with a wink.

"Are you sure you can handle it?" she teased back.

"Give me your best shot."

She chuckled as she led me into the store. We perused for a few minutes before she grabbed something off the rack across from me and ran to the dressing room without letting me see what it was. I continued browsing while she tried on her item and I found something that she would look beautiful in. It was a blue-green silk floor-length nightgown with strips of black lace. I could imagine the garment transforming her to look like a mermaid emerging from the ocean. While she was changing I decided to buy it for her as a surprise.

She came out a minute later with whatever it was she found hiding behind her back.

"Turn around. I don't want you to see what I'm buying. That takes all the fun out of it."

"Well, I wouldn't say that, but I'll wait for you outside."

When I left the shop, I glanced down at my watch and saw that it was already noon. That was perfect. We could make a quick stop by the liquor store for some day drinks and then be on our way. Savannah came out and we made our stop. She got an Arizona tea and some apricot rum shots and I got a coke and rum shot that we mixed together. As soon as we had our drinks we were off to the carnival.

We walked around, taking everything in. I thought to myself that I had to win something for her before the day was over, but first, I thought, a ride.

"Which ride do you want to go on first, beautiful?"

"You."

I busted out laughing at the cheesy line. "How about that will be the last ride of the day?"

"Well, fine. How about the Ferris wheel?"

As the Ferris wheel started up, I looked over at her, thinking about how lucky I was. When we got to the top, I kissed her with everything I felt for her. We broke away breathless and took in the city before us. Live music from below drifted up to us making the day even more special.

The day continued on perfectly, with us going on ride after ride, smiling and laughing as we went. Before long, we got hungry and decided on some turkey legs and beer. We of course had a sword fight with our turkey legs before we dug into them, then got a funnel cake with extra powdered sugar to top it off.

"You look cute all covered in powdered sugar," I said.

"I'm not covered in powdered sugar," she said, looking a little confused.

"You are now!" I said, laughing as I sprinkled the sugar from our dessert over her head.

"Hey!" she yelled, chasing after me.

When she finally caught up to me, I wrapped my arms around her and kissed her deeply.

"Mmm. It tastes even sweeter on you."

Before things could get too heated, I broke away and looked for a booth where I could win her something. I stopped in front of a ring toss booth.

"Oh, shit yes. I am going to own this game and win you that unicorn!"

"Oooh. Okay. I love unicorns. It's so fluffy!"

I bought into the game and sure enough, got her the unicorn. She squealed when I gave it to her. The last thing that we did was get our faces painted. I decided to go with a tiger, and Savannah went all out and got Day of the Dead.

"Wow, this might sound weird, but you would make a really sexy skeleton," I said, admiring how hot she was all painted up.

"Ha! You're just trying to get some when we get back to my place."

"Well, that is true, but remember, you asked to ride me," I reminded her.

"Oh, I haven't forgotten, baby, but I don't think that we should let this awesome face paint go to waste. Do you want to go out for a drink or something?"

"Sure, honey. Do you want to get dinner while we're at it? I'm sure we will work up our appetites later. We may as well get ahead of the ball."

"Good idea," she said, winking at me.

We decided on The Highland Tavern. They were a pretty chill bar and they had good food and drinks. We got a table and ordered some drinks and burgers. After our drinks came, we took a look around.

"Oh, shit! They have ping-pong, Charlie! You are so gonna get your ass kicked!" Savannah exclaimed as soon as she spotted the tables.

"We'll see, pretty lady."

As we started playing, we discovered that we were pretty evenly matched. About ten minutes into the match we had a crowd of people watching and cheering us on. We went back and forth, both of us almost winning multiple times, but then, sure enough, on the millionth game point, she served me a curve ball, and beat me. The crowd went crazy as soon as Savannah screamed, and threw her hands in the air with victory. I chuckled as I made my way over to her.

"I told you I was going to beat you."

"Yes you did, but I want a rematch as soon as we're done eating our burgers," I said, kissing her deeply and leading her back to our table.

Our burgers were lukewarm when we got to the table, due to the fact that we took so long playing, but we dug in anyway, neither of us realizing how hungry we were. I looked up and watched her eat for a moment, thinking to myself how much I liked that she wasn't shy about eating with gusto in front of me. That was one of my biggest pet peeves about women. They were too self-conscious about their weight, and what they should eat in front of other people. Savannah wasn't like that at all, and it was very refreshing. Plus, it made her body fill out in all of the perfect places.

After we finished eating and ordered another round of drinks, I challenged her to a rematch. After another twenty-minute round, I finally won. I did the Aaron Rodgers belt move, making Savannah laugh, and then made her give me a victory kiss. We took off for her place soon after, both of us tired from the exciting day.

"I would like to make love to you when we get home and then have you fall asleep in my arms," I said to her as we pulled out of the spot, and headed toward her house.

"Hey, I have no objection to that. Although, I would like to try on my new lingerie for you."

"Well, I better get you home quick then," I said, making her chuckle.

"Today has been the perfect day. Thank you so much for sharing it with me."

"It was my pleasure, Savannah," I said, taking my eyes off the road to smile at her.

I parked the car and opened the door for her, giving her my hand to help her out. She thanked me as we made our way to her front door. As soon as the door closed behind us, I was attacking her mouth. I pushed her up against the wall as she dropped her purse, wrapping her arms around my neck and attempting to climb up my body. I grabbed her by the ass, hoisting her up, and pressed my growing erection against her. She moaned into my mouth as I ground shamelessly against her.

"Charlie, hold on. I want to wear my new outfit for you," she said breathlessly.

"Okay, baby, but be quick. I don't think I can last much longer without being inside you," I said, stepping away from her and smacking her ass as she grabbed her bag, and scurried off to the bedroom.

I looked down to see Jorge rubbing against my leg in greeting. I reached down to pet him, and he was soon purring. I took a quick peek in his food bowl to see if it was empty. Sure enough. I decided to feed him while Savannah was getting ready. After I was done, I went to the bathroom to wash off the face paint from earlier. Just as I finished, Savannah opened the door to her bedroom. She too had washed off her face paint.

She looked like Aphrodite in ivory and champagne lace. There were candles lit in the room behind her, and she was wearing a tight-fitted baby doll and black heels, making her legs look impossibly long. Her barely concealed nipples were hard and peeking out through the fabric, and my mouth watered, needing to taste them.

"Hey, stud. I think I'm ready for my ride now," she said seductively.

"Oh, baby, I'll give you more than just a ride."

"Oh really? Does that include a spanking? 'Cause while I look innocent, I've been a bad girl," she told me, making my erection strain against the buttons of my jeans.

"Well, you were a good girl telling me about it, so how about I punish you first, and then reward you for your honesty?" I took a step toward her, feeling like I was stalking my prey.

"Oh, yes please," she begged, turning to go back into the bedroom.

Once she reached the bed she climbed onto it on all fours and looked back at me. I groaned at the vision of her perfect ass in front of me to do whatever I wanted with.

As soon as I got to her, I palmed her and moved her nightie up, exposing her underwear-clad butt to me.

"Well, I think these will be the first to go," I said, slowly dragging the lace panties down her legs. As soon as they were off her I went back to squeezing her ass. "You want me to spank you, Savannah? Beg me."

"Please, Charlie. I like it rough. I want to feel the sting of your palm on my tight ass."

I groaned again at her words, letting go of my reservations. I brought my hand up and spanked her.

"Harder," she moaned.

I swatted her much harder this time, and when she squirmed toward me for more I hit her five more times in quick succession. When I pulled away, I looked down, seeing my red handprints all over her bottom. I gently soothed the skin with my mouth, taking away the hurt and turning it into heat as my fingers went to her pussy, finding her completely soaked and dripping down her legs.

"Oh fuck, baby, you are such a dirty girl. Do you want more?" I asked.

"Yes. I want my ass stinging as you fuck me from behind."

I gave her what she wanted, spanking her until we lost track of time, and by the time we were both panting from sexual need, I finally gave in to what we both wanted, undoing my pants and plunging into her wet heat. We both groaned at the sensation.

"This is going to be over quickly, but I promise you another round after this," I said, pounding mercilessly into her.

She whimpered as I reached underneath her to grasp a nipple in between my fingertips, twisting and tugging it harshly.

"Touch yourself, Savannah. Show me how naughty you are," I whispered in her ear, then tugged her earlobe between my teeth.

I could feel her pussy clamp down on my cock as soon as her fingers brushed against her clit, and I knew she was close. I pumped into her faster and tugged on her nipple and ear at the same time, and she detonated around me.

"Fuck, Savannah. You're going to make me come. Keep clenching around my dick."

A few thrusts later, and I came deep inside her tight body. I caught my breath for a moment before I kissed her back and slid gently out of her. I undressed, and lay in the bed next to her, pulling her close to me.

"Just give me another minute, baby, and I will make love to you this time," I said, stroking my fingers up and down her back.

"Okay," she said easily, relaxing into my embrace.

We stayed like that for a while, just content to be in each other's arms. It was nice being this comfortable with each other. It just felt easy. I hoped she felt the same way.

When I had finally caught my breath, I rolled her onto her back, and gently undressed her. I then brought my mouth to hers, kissing her deeply. She was lazy with it at first, but after a minute she started responding. I pulled away to drop kisses on her neck and down her body. I stopped at her breasts to pay special attention to her nipples. When she was squirming, I continued on my journey downward, making sure to dip my tongue into her belly button. I finally reached her mound, nipping across it gently.

"Charlie, you're killing me!"

I chuckled as I latched my lips around her clit. She cried out as I sucked her nub into my mouth. She tasted sweet, salty, and delicious. I would never get enough of her. I groaned at her flavor, and it seemed to get her even more excited. I scraped my facial hair along the length of her pussy, my tongue following, and inserted two of my fingers inside her. She immediately drenched my digits and clenched around the invasion. I pumped her a few times, before dragging my index finger toward her back entrance. She tensed.

"Savannah, baby, just relax. I promise, I'll be gentle and you'll love it."

She took a few deep breaths, and I distracted her with my tongue some more. When she finally relaxed, I very gently pushed against the tight ring of muscle. It resisted for just a moment before she let me in. I slowly dragged my finger in and out, making sure to suck her hard and fast to keep her out of her own head. After about a minute she seemed to start really enjoying it, and even started pushing herself harder onto my hand. Another minute, and she was screaming her release, and clenching around me.

I didn't give her any time to come down before I was sliding into her soaked cunt. As soon as I was fully inside her she opened her eyes to look into mine, further cementing our connection.

"Make love to me, Charlie. I trust you."

Her words flipped a switch and I let loose, plunging slowly, but purposefully, deep inside of her. I wanted her to feel every single inch of me for days to come.

This time was different for us. There was no race to the finish line, we just took pleasure and gave pleasure, reveling in each other's bodies. Her legs were wrapped around my back, pulling me deeper with every thrust, and her hands caressing my back and hair. I lowered my head, and sucked her piercing into my mouth, laving it with my tongue.

She was moaning incoherently by the time she said, "Yes, Charlie. I'm going to come again. Make me come."

I ground my pelvis against her clit as I thrust the deepest yet, and bit down gently on her nipple, feeling her tight pussy clutching my cock over and over as she rode out her orgasm. Hers set mine off and I looked into her eyes as I came. After it was over, I looked down at her and said something that I'd never said to anyone.

"Savannah, I think I'm falling in love with you."

Chapter 17

Savannah

Three months later...

I woke with Charlie's arm wrapped around me and his morning wood pressed into my ass. I smiled to myself thinking about how perfect the past few months had been. Ever since that night he told me he was falling for me, he rarely left my apartment. We weren't "technically" living together, because let's face it, I still didn't quite have my shit together, but we weren't far off. I still hadn't told him I loved him. I did of course, but something about vocalizing it had me scared shitless.

I had also opened up to him about my past. That happened around a month or two into us dating. He had done as he promised, and hadn't pushed me on any of it, which I can only imagine was super difficult. I know I would've been curious. I told him everything, about Greg and about my parents. It hadn't been easy, and I'm pretty sure that I had been ugly crying for most of it, but I was very glad that I had, and that the conversation was over. It had just been something that I had to tell him one day, and here he still was. I smiled to myself thinking about how lucky I was. Of course those conversations had triggered flashbacks for me, giving me nightmares for a couple days after I told him. One in particular really bothered me.

It was one of those rare days, where Greg and I were actually having a nice time together. He woke up in a fantastic mood that morning, and we spent the day just hanging out around the house.

"Hey, do you wanna go to dinner tonight?" I asked. "We haven't gone to our favorite place in a while." Our favorite place being the Chinese restaurant down the street from our apartment.

"Sure, babe," he replied.

That night we had a nice dinner, laughing together and talking about random stuff, work mostly. We both had a couple drinks and walked back home, holding hands. Maybe things were starting to take a turn for us, I thought.

As soon as we got into the bedroom to change, Greg started kissing me and roughly groping me. Normally, I would be excited by the attention, but that night I had developed a big headache from the alcohol I had with dinner. I pulled away from him.

"Honey, I'm sorry but I'm not really in the mood tonight. I have a huge headache from the wine," I told him.

"Oh, baby, you'll feel better as soon as you have my cock in your mouth," he groaned against my neck.

"Greg, come on, I'm really not in the mood."

"Are you fucking kidding me, Savannah? You've been a little cock tease all day and now all the sudden you're just not in the mood? God, you can be such a bitch sometimes," he said, taking off his shirt and angrily throwing it into the hamper. "Why don't you think about someone other than yourself for a goddamn minute and give me what I need from you, huh?"

I looked at him, not understanding what he was telling me. It felt like he had slapped me right across the face. I always tried to give him what he needed, but apparently that wasn't the case.

"Okay, Greg, we can have sex. I'll give you what you need," I told him, even though now the thought of being with him had formed a rock in the pit

of my stomach.

He quickly shoved both of our pants down and pushed me facedown onto the bed. Before I knew it, he was roughly thrusting into me. Since I was not aroused, I was dry and it was very painful. I tucked my face into the comforter beneath me, tears leaking from my eyes.

Within minutes, he finished, stilling inside me. Without saying a word, he pulled out of me, put some pants on, and lay down on his side of the bed, immediately going to sleep. I pulled mine back up before climbing onto my side and crying myself to sleep.

The night I had that nightmare, I woke up, jolting out of bed and looking next to me, relieved to see Charlie sleeping soundly, instead of my ex. I had lain back down and cuddled up next to him, and he stirred before wrapping his arms tightly around me, the steady sound of his heart beating beneath my ear lulling me back to sleep.

I put all thoughts of that night aside as I stretched my arms above my head, yawning, and looked at the clock. It was 8:00 a.m. Charlie had to work late the night before and didn't get in until around 3:00 a.m. Luckily we both had the day off, so I let him sleep while I got up and did some stuff around the house.

Jorge of course wanted breakfast as soon as I got out of bed, so I fed him and then took a shower. As I was drying off, my phone rang on the countertop.

Mom.

Shit. I debated answering. I hadn't talked to her since my dad got out, and I had told her I wasn't going to be there. I decided to let it go to voice mail to see what she wanted. By the time I got dressed and had my hair in a French braid, I still wasn't quite ready to listen to the message, so I started cleaning the apartment. That was always my go-to when something made me anxious.

After about an hour of cleaning, I had pretty much the whole apartment done, and I was feeling marginally better. I decided to woman up and just listen to the damn message.

"Savannah, darling, it's your mother. I know we haven't spoken for a while, but I was hoping that you might want to come over for dinner tonight. You haven't seen your father or me in a very long time, and I think that it's time you came over. In fact, I haven't seen you since your father went to court the first time and that is just unacceptable. We miss you and hope you can make it tonight. Please call me back to let me know."

Well, that was unexpected. I had no idea how I felt about the message. I never thought that my mother would leave me something like that. She did of course layer it with something only she could, lots of guilt and topped it off with scolding, but underneath it all, it sounded like she actually wanted to see me.

Was I seriously thinking about going? I could bring Charlie, and he could meet my parents. Jesus. That was such a terrible idea. That would have him running for the hills in about two seconds flat. It would be something that would have to happen eventually though, right?

"Savannah, baby, why are you pacing? You only pace when something is wrong," Charlie asked me, coming out of the bedroom and into the living room.

"My mother called."

I watched surprise flicker over his face before he asked, "Well, what did she say?"

"She wants me to come over for dinner tonight."

"Are you going to?" he asked.

"I don't know. I haven't seen my parents in over five years," I said, pausing while I tried to gather my thoughts. "If I did go, would you come with me?"

"You want me to meet them?"

"Well, not if you don't want to. Never mind. It was a stupid idea anyway."

"Hey. Stop. Baby, I would love to come with you. I'm just surprised is all. Of course I'll be there. Plus, I've been curious about them for a while, and it's something that I feel like we need to do. I would like to experience all the aspects of your life. Even the ones you don't like so much."

I breathed a sigh of relief and I smiled at him, leaning in for a kiss. Before I could overthink it, I called my mother. It rang twice before she answered.

"Savannah, darling. How are you? I didn't think you would call me back."

"Yeah, hi, Mom. I thought about it and I can do dinner tonight."

"Really? Honey, that's lovely to hear! I know your father will really love to see you as well."

"Yeah, I'm sure he'll be thrilled," I said sarcastically. "Listen, Mom, I'm going to bring my boyfriend, Charlie, with me tonight."

"You're dating someone? Why didn't you tell me?"

"Well, we haven't been the closest since I left home," I said.

"And whose fault is that?" she asked, in only a way that she could, trying to make me feel like shit for not keeping in close contact. I took a deep breath to compose myself before I said something rude or hung up on her.

"Yeah, I know, Mom. Do you want us to come over for dinner or not?"

"Yes of course, dear. When did you get so sensitive? Be here at seven sharp."

"Aye aye, Captain," I said sarcastically. I couldn't help it. My family brought out the worst in me.

"Savannah," my mother reprimanded, "I taught you better than that. Now stop being so rude."

"Yes, Mother." I rolled my eyes. "I'll see you tonight."

After we hung up, I looked over at Charlie to see him barely holding in a chuckle. While I'd been on the phone he had made coffee, and he held out a mug for me. He knew exactly how I liked it. Strong with lots of hazelnut creamer. I sighed in delight as I took a big drink of it.

"So, how did it go?" he asked.

"Well, tonight should be interesting. You need to be prepared. My parents are horribly judgmental. Plus, they haven't seen me since I put red in my hair, pierced a whole lot of shit, and got a fuckton of tattoos."

"Not to mention the fact that you're dating a scruffy, tattooed fireman," he said, teasing me. "I'm curious to see how they take me."

"Well, I am going to apologize on their behalf ahead of time because, as stated before, my parents are judgmental assholes," I said, feeling increasingly nervous the more I thought about how tonight was going to go down.

"Savannah, I love you, and no matter how tonight goes or what your parents say, that isn't going to change. Okay?"

"Yeah. Okay." I took a deep breath, forcing myself to calm down. My anxiety at times like this was always an inconvenience. I would have to get it under control if I was ever going to survive this night.

We had made the one hour drive to my parents' house just outside of Fort Collins and I still hadn't calmed down at all. Instead, the closer we got to the house, the more I felt like hyperventilating. It helped that I was the one driving. If I hadn't been, I probably would have thrown up already.

I pulled up and parked the car where I always used to. I looked at the old white three-story colonial house with mixed feelings. It was so strange being back here. Some of my memories were fond, but most of them were tainted with guilt and expectations. So much had changed, yet everything was the same. The paint was still the same, along with the blue door. My old tree swing hung innocently from the tree at the very front of the house. While the outside looked the same, I was sure my mother had changed plenty inside. On second thought, maybe she hadn't, considering they didn't have any money left.

I took a deep breath and got out of the car, smoothing my dress down. Apparently, I still wanted to look nice, knowing that my mother would not like it if I showed up in jeans and a T-shirt. Embarrassingly, it took me way too long to get ready before coming here. I spent about half an hour in front of my closet trying to decide what to wear. I finally decided on a purple V-neck dress, fitted on top, flaring out at the waist just under the thick black belt, and ending just above the knee. For my hair I decided to pin the top portion back, and curl the bottom. Overall, I think I did pretty well with my look, considering the way Charlie growled and crushed his lips to mine as soon as I came out of the bedroom.

I came around the outside of the car, and Charlie met me halfway, grabbing my hand and squeezing it.

"Look at you. You're more nervous than I am. Isn't it supposed to be the other way around?" he asked, trying to cheer me up. I guess it was working a little bit.

"Yeah, good point. Anytime you want to switch with me, just let me know," I said, smiling at him.

We got to the front door and I held my hand up to knock, but the door opened before I had the chance to. My mother stood there in all her glory. Full face of makeup that looked professionally done, dressed to the nines in a white pantsuit with a navy silk blouse, and her black six-inch stilettos. Oh, and don't forget the pearl necklace, earrings, and bracelet, all for just a family dinner.

"Savannah, honey, it's so good to see you! And this Charlie of yours! I can't believe you finally found someone to put up with you." I guess she couldn't see me very well yet on the dim porch because she still hadn't commented on my appearance. "Come in, you two!"

As soon as we stepped inside with proper lighting, she inhaled sharply as her eyes raked over every inch of me and then made their same perusal of Charlie. I looked over at him to see him appearing unaffected, standing tall and smiling.

"Mrs. Ajax, my name is Charlie. It's nice to finally meet you."

She looked down at his outstretched hand, the one with all the tattoos on it, before looking up at him and pasting a fake smile on her face as she reluctantly stuck out a perfectly manicured hand to shake his.

"Yes, you too." I don't think she had ever said less to someone in her life. She turned her attention back to me. "Savannah, what did you do to yourself?"

"Jesus, Mom. You can't even make it one minute before starting in on me? We're just here for you both to meet Charlie and to have an uneventful dinner."

"I just don't understand why you would do all of this to yourself. You used to be so beautiful. Now you're covered in tattoos and piercings and your hair is all messed up. Not to mention all of the weight you've gained. You lost your perfect figure, darling."

"Mrs. Ajax, I understand that Savannah looks much different from when you last saw her, but she is the most gorgeous, kind woman I have ever met, and if you don't stop belittling her right now, we will leave. I will not allow you to talk about her like that, even if you are her mother," Charlie said, his tone stern but polite.

My mother stared at him like a deer caught in headlights. She was silent for about thirty seconds, looking between the two of us before replying.

"Very well then. Let's go see your father, dear. He's in the living room watching TV."

I took a deep breath, looking at Charlie to find him smiling softly at me and squeezing my hand in encouragement.

"Don't listen to a word she said. You are the most beautiful woman I have ever seen, and I love all of your luscious curves. It gives me something to grab on to when I'm deep inside of you," Charlie whispered in my ear as he grabbed my ass while my mother wasn't looking, his voice getting rougher as he spoke, effectively making me feel sexy, wanted, and turned on all at the same time.

We followed my mother into the living room where my dad was in his chair, his eyes glued to the baseball game.

"Paul, darling, Savannah and her friend Charlie are here."

"Mom, he's not my friend. Charlie is my boyfriend," I said, not able to ignore her dig, especially after how Charlie had just stuck up for me.

My dad didn't even glance up from the TV. "Just a minute. It's almost done," he said. Wow, that was great. He hadn't seen his only daughter in over five years, and he couldn't even be bothered to look at me.

"Okay, darling. Well, we will be waiting in the dining room while you finish. We would like it if you would join us when you are done," my mother replied.

"Sharon, I can't hear the damn game. Go wherever you want, as long as you aren't in here."

We hastily went to the dining room, which I was grateful for considering that's where the bar was located. I made a beeline for the booze, quickly pouring myself a big glass of red wine, and Charlie two fingers of scotch. He gratefully took his and we took large drinks before sitting down opposite my mom. She was quiet for a minute and the silence stretched on awkwardly.

"Well, Paul will be here soon and then we can start in on dinner," she said, trying to look unaffected. I guess I never paid attention or realized when I was younger, but my dad treated her like shit. Maybe that was part of the reason that she was always so hard on me. For the first time, maybe ever, I felt sorry for her. Why did she stay with him and support him when he was so clearly awful and unworthy?

We awkwardly made small talk for a bit as we waited for my father to come in so we could eat.

"So, darling, what have you been doing with your life since I last saw you?" she asked.

"Well, I moved to Denver, and I've been building my clientele at the tattoo shop that I'm at. I've actually gotten pretty busy and am starting to book out in advance. I've been dating this guy for about three months," I said, nudging Charlie next to me and smiling at him.

"Well, that's interesting," she said, looking completely uninterested in everything I just said. "Oh, you know who I ran into the other day? Grace Porter from your high school, dear. She's married to a lawyer and she gets to stay at home with the children. She looked like she was doing pretty well for herself. Isn't that wonderful?"

I could feel my jaw clenching harder with each word she said. When she was finished, I took a deep breath and let it out. I just needed to get through this one night.

"Yes, Mother. That's fantastic," I said, trying my hardest not to get too worked up.

After about ten minutes my dad waltzed in, looking every bit the politician he used to be.

"Hello, Savannah. Long time no see" was all he said. No hug or anything.

"Hello, Father." If he wanted to be short with me, I could do the same. "This is my boyfriend, Charlie."

"Hello, sir. Thank you for having me over for dinner," Charlie said as he shook my dad's hand.

My father looked so uninterested it was almost laughable. He didn't reply at all, just sat down and started loading up his dinner plate with the salad that we were starting with. For a while we ate in uncomfortable silence. I didn't even know what to say to my parents anymore. I didn't know them and they didn't know me. I was a completely different person than the last time that I saw them. They were still of course the same people, but I now viewed them in a completely different light.

After the salad, we started on the main course—mashed potatoes, roast beef, and rolls. I loaded my plate up with everything, including extra potatoes. After I finished serving myself, I looked up to see my mother staring at me with a disapproving look on her face, no doubt because I didn't stop at the salad and loaded my plate with lots of carbs. I looked at her plate to see only a small piece of the roast beef.

"Savannah, honey, don't you think that you put a little too much on your plate?" she asked me. I knew it.

"Nope. Thanks, Mother," I said, bitterly, deliberately loading more stuff onto my plate just to piss her off.

"I love Savannah's appetite. I think most women today are too concerned about their weight. Not to mention how beautiful her curves are," Charlie said, smiling at me.

That seemed to shut my mother up on that subject, because all she said was "Hmmm."

"So Charlie, what do you do?" my mother asked.

"Oh, I'm a fireman."

"Probably couldn't get any other job with all that hair and all those tattoos," my father said disdainfully.

"Excuse me?" I asked, my face heating as my temper rose even further than before.

"I just mean that no respectable place of business would hire someone while they looked like that."

"Oh, so you can't be a bad person or a bad worker if you look like you do? You can't sell drugs or ruin people's lives and lie to every single person you know if you cut your hair short and wear a fucking suit?

And you can't be a respectable person with a good job if you have long hair and a beard and tattoos? Is that what you're saying, Dad?" I said, not able to hold my tongue anymore. They could demean me all they wanted, but they had no right to attack Charlie. He was such a good man and he didn't deserve any of this.

"Savannah! Don't talk to your father that way." This came from my mother.

"Are you fucking kidding me?" I asked, looking incredulously at her, not believing my own ears. I knew she backed him up in everything, especially in the public eye, but this? "You both are terrible. Charlie is such a good man, and Dad, being a fireman is a very noble profession. He helps people. He *rescues* people. Do you not understand that or just not care? You think just because he doesn't make lots of money and buy a big fancy house that he isn't someone who is worthy? Jesus. I can't believe that I was made by the two of you."

"It just figures that this is what you would do with your life. You were supposed to make me look good and maybe follow in my footsteps one day. You were going to go to an Ivy League school and actually do something with your life. And look at you now. So successful as a tattoo artist with your gangbanger-looking boyfriend. I'm ashamed to be your father," he said, contempt dripping from his lips.

"You're ashamed? You've got nothing on me, Dad. Actually, I should thank you for fucking up so bad and going to prison. It really opened my eyes to what horrible people you are, and showed me that I could do whatever I wanted, as opposed to just what everyone else always wanted. I am more successful being a tattoo artist in my tiny apartment than you will ever be, Dad, and that's because I am happy doing what I do, and I don't give a shit what anyone else thinks about me. Especially you. So, thank you."

"You know, I love how you're so upset with me, but you don't put any of the blame on your mother. You haven't talked to me since I was arrested but you had no problem giving her your new number," he snapped at me.

"Well, she's not the one who committed the crime now, is she? I still have no idea why the fuck she stands by you after all you've done."

"Oh, she may not have technically committed the crime, but she is just as guilty, if not more so."

"Paul!" my mother exclaimed, looking frantic. My eyes flicked between the two of them as I tried to figure out what was going on.

"What is that supposed to mean? She didn't find out about the fact that you were dealing drugs until you were arrested, same as me," I questioned.

"Oh, Savannah. So naive. Is that what she told you? It was your mother's idea the whole time, dear. The campaign wasn't going as well as we thought it would, and she didn't want to have to give up all of her nice things that were paid for from the money that we did make. She was behind the whole thing. She's the fucking reason I went to prison in the first place. Her and her greed," he finished, looking at my mother with so much disdain, she should've gone up in flames.

"What? Is that true?" I asked, looking at her for answers. Her face told me all I needed to know. I stood up, throwing my napkin on the table as Charlie did the same. "It was a mistake coming here tonight. All I wanted was for Charlie to see another part of me and meet my parents, and maybe try to get past what had happened between us, but it's clear that's never going to happen. I don't know why I haven't realized what kind of people you both are until now. Well, never again. Have a nice life."

Charlie and I walked out, not looking back at my parents, even when my mother started calling my name. As we neared the car, Charlie took the keys from me, knowing that I would be in no condition to drive. As soon as we got into the car and on the road, I pulled the emergency double shot of tequila from my purse and downed it. I took a few deep breaths as I closed my eyes.

Well, as far as how I thought tonight would go, that was the worst-case scenario. Except for maybe them calling the cops. At least it was over with and I didn't have to see them or talk to them ever again. And I wouldn't. I didn't want to have anything to do with either of them for the rest of my life. They might be my parents, but they were not good people.

Charlie let me stew for about ten minutes or so, when he finally grabbed my hand, bringing my attention to him.

"Savannah, I know I already told you this earlier, but I'm going to tell you again because I feel like you need to hear it. I love you. This does not change anything between us, except for me feeling closer to you. We got through this night together and we never have to do it again. I think you are so brave for standing up to them like that. Thank you for speaking up for me. No one has done that for me in a long time," he said, and I was overcome with emotion. That made the whole shitty night worth it right there. "I am so sorry that they hid so much from you, and that you got stuck with them for your parents, but they aren't your family. You get to choose your family, and from what I've seen, you've chosen well. Anna, Lauren, and me. We're your family. And we love you. No matter what."

"Pull over," I said. Charlie looked at me questioningly before doing as I asked, getting off the highway and pulling off onto an unpaved road. I climbed onto his lap as soon as he put the car into park. "I love you, Charlie." I heard his sharp inhale at my declaration. "You are worth sticking up for. I know I still have my hang-ups, but I am doing my best to work through them because you are worth it," I told him, grabbing his face and looking into his eyes. We said more in that look than we ever could out loud, and our connection was solidified.

I couldn't take it anymore. I pulled his face to mine and I kissed him with everything I felt. I poured all of my love, appreciation, and awe for him into that kiss. Within seconds I felt him harden underneath me. I moaned as I ground myself against him, grateful that I was wearing a dress. I broke the kiss to reach down and unbuckle his belt, although it was difficult because his lips had moved to my cleavage and were very distracting.

As soon as I got his pants undone, I closed my fingers around his length, stroking him from root to tip. He groaned against me and I felt the vibrations deep in my chest. He reached up and pulled my tit outside of my dress as he latched his mouth around my nipple. My moan echoed through the car as his teeth bit down gently and tugged. His fingers made their way up my thigh before finally finding the edge of my panties, tracing along the seam before dipping inside to find my wet center. We stroked each other until we were panting, needy messes.

"Charlie, I need you. Right now," I pleaded.

"I know, baby. Me too," he said as he moved my panties to the side and plunged forcefully into me.

We both groaned at the delicious contact. My lips found their way back to his as his hands guided my hips up and down onto him. The tension from the entire night had me so pent-up that I was already on the verge of exploding.

"Charlie, I'm close already," I panted.

He grunted as he doubled his efforts. He moved my hips faster and harder over his, plunging his cock so deep inside of me. His fingers pressed against my clit, as his other hand reached back to finger my asshole after gathering the moisture from my drenched pussy. As soon as his thick finger pressed inside I detonated, clenching around him.

"Fuck, Savannah. Look at me," he breathed.

I brought my eyes to his, and the look in them already had me building again.

"Tell me again. I need to hear it," he said.

"I love you, Charlie. So much," I said, staring right into his soul. The words sent him over the edge as he came deep inside me. His orgasm and the look on his face spiraled me into another mind-bending climax.

Chapter 18

Charlie

I woke up to my alarm at 5:30 a.m. with Savannah wrapped around me like a vine. After we got home the night before, we made love again in her bed before we fell asleep draped around each other. She was feeling really needy when we got back from the dinner, understandably, and I didn't mind at all catering to her needs.

I shut my alarm off, disentangling myself from my girl, and making my way toward the bathroom to get ready for work. Five minutes into my shower, Savannah came in with me.

"Baby, what are you doing up so early? You don't have to work today," I asked.

"I know, but I missed you, and I wanted to see you before you left me alone all day with my thoughts," she said, sounding lonely already as she pressed herself against me from behind for a hug.

"Oh, honey, I'm sorry. I wish I could just stay in bed with you all day, but I have to work in forty-five minutes."

"I know. I just wanted to be with you," she said, grabbing the soap and working it between her hands to create a lather.

She set the soap down and ran her hands all over my body, cleaning

130

me thoroughly. When she got to my back she dug her thumbs into my shoulders, kneading my tight muscles. I moaned as she made her way up to my neck.

"That feels so good, Savannah."

"Good. You need it. Your shoulders are very tight. No wonder you get so many headaches," she said. "Now turn around. I'm not finished cleaning you."

I did and she soaped up once more, bringing her hands to my chest. She washed under my arms and then slowly went down to my stomach in circular motions, dipping her finger into my belly button. After my chest and stomach were cleaned to her satisfaction she moved her hands lower, wrapping her fingers around my cock.

"Honey, I don't have time to give you the attention you need."

"I know, Charlie. You don't need to. I want to give you this before you go to work. I don't need anything else."

I deliberated, hating leaving her hanging, but then her fingers squeezed around me again, making my decision for me.

"Okay, but we have to make this quick because I can't be late."

"Oh, I know how to make you come. Or did you forget?" she asked, squeezing me tighter.

She got down on her knees, getting both of her hands in on the action, pumping and twisting.

"Wash the soap off so that I can use my mouth," she demanded.

After I was finished, she popped me into her mouth, quickly and forcefully sucking me. Her hand latched on to my balls as she gently massaged them. Within a few minutes she had me ready to explode. As though she knew I was close, she switched it up, bringing her mouth to my balls and wrapping her strong hands around my length, switching between faster and slower strokes to keep me on edge.

"Savannah, baby, I'm close. Where do you want me to come?"

Instead of answering me, she once again wrapped her beautiful lips around my cock and sucked hard, sending me over the edge into a very intense and quick orgasm. I shot down her throat and she looked up at me as I did, her eyes tearing a bit from my cum.

When she swallowed all of me down, she stood up, getting some water on her hands before splashing some on her face. She turned around to kiss me before getting out of the shower. I quickly finished washing before getting out and drying myself off. I went to the bedroom to put my clothes on to find Savannah lying in bed already passed out again; she hadn't even gotten dressed before crawling back in. I pulled the covers over her before kissing her cheek.

I left her a note saying that I loved her and that I would be home at three. I grabbed my keys and locked the door on my way out (she had a key made for me after about a month into our relationship, since I was over every night anyway).

Work was slow that day. We did have a few calls, but all very minor and pretty uneventful. I decided to call Savannah on my lunch break to see how she was doing. She should have been up since it was around eleven.

"Hey, baby," she answered on the third ring.

"Hi, sweetie. How's everything going?"

"It's fine. Just cleaning a bit. I need to go to the grocery store, but I don't really feel like it."

"Well, if you want to wait for me to get off work we can go together," I said.

"Really? Okay. I would much rather go with you. Just don't dawdle a bunch like you did last time. And you bought way too much junk food," she teased.

"Hey, I don't dawdle. I just like to go down all the aisles to make sure I'm not forgetting anything," I said, laughing.

"Well, fine, but this time we are shopping my way."

"Yes, ma'am," I said sarcastically, knowing that it would annoy her.

"I'll see you tonight," she said as she huffed and hung up, making me chuckle.

I pushed through the rest of my workday, just wanting to be home with her. I knew she would be fine after what happened with her parents, but I still wanted to be there to comfort her.

My shift was finally over and I was able to head home to her. As soon as I walked in the door, I was greeted with the smell of chemicals. She had deep cleaned the whole apartment. I knew it was her go-to when she was upset, but I didn't realize she was this upset.

"Savannah? Where are you?"

"I'm in the kitchen!" she yelled.

I made my way to her, but when I got to the kitchen she was nowhere to be found. All I saw was a huge stack of old food and random other things in a huge pile right behind the open pantry door. As I went around to the other side, I saw Savannah sitting on the floor of the pantry, digging through the bottom shelf.

"Are you looking for something, Sweetie?"

"No, smartass. I'm cleaning out the pantry. I've been meaning to do this for months," she said.

"Well, the apartment looks really good. Have you been cleaning all day?" I asked.

"Pretty much. I made coffee with Baileys this morning, and an egg on toast with avocado, and then I started cleaning," she said, throwing more stuff on the pile.

"Well, aren't you hungry? You must be if that's all you've had to eat today."

"No, not really. I just want to finish this and then we can go grocery shopping."

"Baby, you need to eat."

"Well, I don't have much of an appetite," she snapped at me.

"Okay" was all I said. She clearly wasn't in a good mood, so I decided to leave her to it.

I hopped into the shower to wash my day off, letting the steam loosen my muscles and calm me. I stood there just letting the water wash over me for about ten minutes before I soaped up. When I got out, I felt much better. I changed into something clean, and put my hair up in my typical man bun. When I went back into the kitchen, Savannah was just throwing out all the old food. She looked at me as I came in, appearing slightly calmer than before.

"Hey. I'm sorry I snapped at you. I've been in a mood all day, hence the cleaning, and I just haven't felt like eating. I'm still upset about last night, and I shouldn't have taken it out on you," she said. She looked a bit uncomfortable apologizing.

"It's okay, babe. I know you're still upset, and I know you don't feel like it, but you should at least eat a little something. If you don't want to actually eat a meal then maybe you can have like an apple or something to get your blood sugar up. What do you think?"

"Yeah, okay. Let's see what I still have in the fridge before we go shopping," she said, before deciding on a tortilla and some hummus. When she finished it she put the hummus away and then said, "Okay, I'm ready. Let's go to the store."

"Want me to drive?" I asked.

"No, I'm good. I want to drive."

Ten minutes later, we were at King Soopers, wandering the aisles. Savannah hadn't put much in the cart since she still didn't have much of an appetite, so I was glad she waited for me to come with her. I filled the cart with everything I could think of. Lots of fruits and veggies, meat, and only a little bit of junk food.

As we were walking up the dairy aisle, something horrible happened. I was grabbing a jug of milk to put in our cart when someone I really didn't want to see passed by, and a feeling of dread settled in my stomach.

"Charlie?" she asked.

"Brittany? You shouldn't be here," I said.

"Who's this?" Brittany asked disdainfully. "Your new whore that you're cheating on me with, you son of a bitch?! I can't believe you're doing this to me again!"

I turned to Savannah to see her looking horror-struck, before her face erupted into pure rage.

"Savannah, just listen," I said. Before I could say anything else, she slapped me hard across the face.

"You. Mother. Fucker," she said, before she turned and ran off, leaving me standing in the middle of the grocery store, wishing I could rewind the past two minutes.

Chapter 19

Savannah

I ran as quickly as I could out of the store. I was so glad that I drove because otherwise I would have been stuck here with that cheating motherfucker. It took me a minute to get the key into the ignition because my hands were shaking so badly. As soon as I did and got the car started, there was a frantic banging on my window.

"Savannah, wait. Just let me explain," Charlie yelled through my window.

I ignored him as I shoved my gear into reverse, and flew out of there like a bat out of hell. As soon as I was on the road, I looked into the rearview to see him chasing after the car. When I couldn't see him anymore, the tears started falling hard and fast.

I knew I couldn't go home because he would find me there, and the bastard had a stupid key. I decided to stop by the liquor store first, because drowning in a bottle of wine would be the only way to stop crying. As soon as I parked my car, I opened my door and threw up the little that I had managed to get down that day.

After that pit stop, I decided to go to the tattoo shop. It was Monday, so it would be closed and I wouldn't have to deal with anyone, and luckily I had put more food than normal in Jorge's dish, so he would be fine for the night. I locked myself in, bringing a blanket from the car with me, and turned my phone off. Already Charlie had called me seven times. I turned on some angry, sad music as loud as it would go, sat on my tattoo table with my blanket wrapped around myself, and the bottle of wine as my only companion for hours.

It finally started to get dark outside and I still didn't move. When I finished off the bottle of wine, I lay down and tried to go to sleep. My mind wouldn't stop running, and it took me much longer to fall asleep than I wanted. The last thought I had before I drifted off was that as much as I didn't want to admit it, I was much more upset than when I caught Greg.

I woke up to Anna opening the shop, looking very confused as to why there was music playing. It wasn't until she came around the corner that she saw me.

"Holy shit, lady! You scared the fuck out of me!" she exclaimed.

"Sorry. Didn't mean to," I said.

"What the fuck happened to you? Did you sleep here?"

"Yeah. I don't want to talk about it."

"Trouble in paradise? Did you and Charlie have a fight or something? If you did that just means that you get to have really hot makeup sex," she said, teasing.

"Not just a fight. And I don't think the girl I met yesterday would be okay with the makeup sex. He cheated," I said, not able to help myself. I wasn't going to say anything, but I could see she wasn't going to let it drop.

"What?! Who's the bitch he's fucking on the side? I'll cut her. And him."

"Me. I'm the other girl. She called me his 'new whore' and said 'I can't believe you're doing this to me again.'"

"Oh, honey. I'm so sorry." She lost all of her teasing and wrapped me in her arms. I broke at the contact and started bawling again. She just held me for a few minutes, and when I finally settled down, I pulled back.

"Thank you, Anna. I needed that," I said.

"You're welcome," she replied, her eyes slightly teary, which surprised me.

"Okay, well, I will set my station up and get to work."

"Girl, please. First off, it's your day off. Secondly, you look like absolute shit. I love you and everything, but I tell it like it is. Just go home and be with your cat, and stay in bed and watch stupid movies."

"But I don't want to see him. What if he comes to the house?" I asked.

"Just text him and tell him you will leave all of his shit outside of your apartment before work tomorrow, and that he can pick it up when you leave for work and then block his number."

"Yeah, I guess I could do that. All right, fine, I'll face the music and go home. Thanks, bitch," I said sarcastically, really dreading the thought of running into him.

Anna gave me one last hug before I left. I walked out of the shop, and immediately the hairs on the back of my neck stood up. I looked around but didn't see anyone in my vicinity. Weird. I could've sworn I felt someone looking at me or watching me. I was probably just paranoid and worried that Charlie would find me when I really didn't want to see him.

As soon as I got to the apartment I knew he wasn't there, but that he had been recently. I saw a note for me on the counter and immediately crumpled it and threw it in the trash. I didn't want to hear any of his shit excuses. It was always the same with these assholes.

Jorge, sensing my mood, immediately came up to me and started rubbing against my leg in an attempt to make me feel better. I picked him up and fell into my bed cuddling with my kitty, which of course started another crying fit. We fell asleep on the bed for a few hours. I had a dream that Charlie hadn't cheated and everything was the way it was before we saw my parents, but then I woke up and realized that it was all a dream. I decided to get it out of the way and text Charlie. I couldn't put it off any longer. I turned my phone on to see twelve voice mails from Charlie and fifteen texts. I deleted all of them without reading or listening to any. I didn't want to hear it. I just wanted this all to be over with.

I work tomorrow at 10 am. I will be leaving all of your belongings outside of my door. Please come and get them or I will throw everything away. And I would like my key back. AND STOP CALLING ME.

After I sent it, I turned my phone back off and started gathering up all of his shit around my apartment. It was all little stuff. Some clothes. Shampoo. A cell phone charger. I put all of it in a box next to my front door so that I wouldn't forget it in the morning. Jorge and I went to bed at 8:00 p.m.

The next morning, I put his stuff outside my door and went to work. When I got there, I was much more put together than the day before, and when I turned my phone back on I finally had the lady balls to block Charlie's number.

When I got home that night, the box was gone and I breathed a sigh of relief. It was all over.

Chapter 20

Savannah

One week later...

It was my day off, and I was moping around the house yet again. I hadn't left except to go to work and the liquor store. I had lost ten pounds because I had zero appetite, and I did not want to return to the grocery store for fear that I would have a meltdown in the dairy aisle.

At five, I heard knocking at my door. Shit. I hadn't heard from Charlie since I blocked his number. I figured he gave up and went back to his bitchy girlfriend.

"Go away, Charlie! I told you I don't want to fucking see you!" I yelled through the door.

"It's not Charlie, bitch! Let us in before we break down the door!" Anna yelled back.

I rolled my eyes as I opened the door to see Lauren and Anna standing there with lots of goodies.

"We let you wallow in self-pity long enough. We are coming in and spending the night after we go into a food coma and get completely shit-faced, and you can't stop us," Anna said, as she barged in with Lauren right on her heels.

"And we bought you real food, because, honey, you don't look good. You've lost a lot of weight in one week," Lauren said, coming in for a tight hug. "I made my famous lasagna. Well, technically my grandma's famous lasagna, but same difference. It's delicious and you will love it."

"Well, fine. As long as you don't expect me to change or get off the couch," I said as I teared up a little. I had good friends.

Anna came into the living room a minute later bearing plates, a spatula, and a bottle of wine.

"So, are we drinking straight from the bottle, or should I get glasses? I always enjoy the former when I'm very upset," Anna said.

"I'll get us glasses," I said. I felt like drinking straight from the bottle would be even more pathetic.

"So, are you going to finally give us the dirty details?" Lauren asked.

"No."

"Please? We know you're upset, but maybe it'll make you feel better. You haven't talked about it hardly at all. You can't bottle this shit up."

"Don't make me kick you bitches out. 'Cause I will. I will steal the lasagna and wine and kick you right the fuck out," I said, completely straight-faced. I was not in the mood to talk about Charlie. I didn't think I would ever be ready.

Lauren held her hands up in a gesture of surrender. "Okay, girl. I'm sorry I asked. I won't bring it up again." It wasn't until that moment that I realized that she had a brand-new sparkly ring, right on her fucking ring finger.

I grabbed her hand and yanked it in front of my face. "Holy shit! You're engaged?!" I asked.

"The fuck?!" Anna yelled. "I'm like your best friend and you didn't think to tell me?!"

"Okay. Everyone just calm down. Yes, I'm engaged. He proposed for our anniversary. I didn't want to say anything because Savannah has been so upset. I didn't want to rub it in."

"*Oh my God!*" Anna and I both yelled together.

"You bitch! You didn't need to keep it a secret because of my stupid depressed ass. I'm so happy for you!" I said, giving her a big hug.

"Let me see this big rock," Anna insisted.

Lauren held her hand out and on it sat the most unique engagement ring I had ever seen, and it was absolutely stunning.

"You have to tell me the details about your ring. I can't figure out all of the stones in it," I said.

"Well, the main pear-shaped one is green sapphire, and the band is rose gold, and then all of the small stones in the band are smokey quartz," she explained.

"It's so beautiful I want to cry! Can I copy you when I get engaged?" Anna asked jokingly.

We all laughed and I asked her to tell us the story.

"Well, for our anniversary, he surprised me with a night picnic. He had a blanket set up with a bunch of candles on it. We ate and had wine, then when we were lying there looking up at the stars, he told me how much he loves me and then he snuck his arm around me so he could hold the ring in front of my face as he asked me to spend the rest of my life with him." By this time, all three of us were pretty much bawling.

"Lauren, you got lucky, girl. You caught a good one," I told her seriously.

"I know I did," she replied.

"So I know it hasn't been that long, but have you set a date yet?" I asked.

"Well, we've talked about next fall, but nothing is decided. It will probably end up being in Michigan since all our family is out there, but that makes it difficult with planning because I will have to rely on other people to go check things out."

"Yeah, I can imagine. Are you guys wanting to have a big wedding or small?" Anna asked.

"Well, we both have a lot of family so it will probably end up being a big wedding. Part of me just wants to go to the fucking courthouse and not have to plan jack shit, but then the girly side of my brain kicks in and really wants it to be special."

"Oooh. Can we go dress shopping with you?!" Anna yelled.

"Oh, yes please!" I agreed.

"Yes, of course you can. It's not like I have anyone else here that can come with me," Lauren said.

"Hell yes. We will be the ultimate dress-shopping team!" I exclaimed.

For the next few hours, we were typical girls and talked about everything wedding related. We also made some brownies from a mix that we found in the cupboard, and ended up eating the whole thing right out of the pan.

At the end of the night, I fell asleep content, stomach full, and blessed with my best friends.

Chapter 21

Charlie

Three weeks later...

It had been one month since the incident in the grocery store, and things still hadn't resolved. I had called and texted Savannah many times, to no avail. I even left her that letter in her apartment to explain, and I still hadn't heard from her. I was trying to give her space, but I was getting really frustrated. The one time that I had used my key to go into her apartment to leave her that note, I felt wrong entering her private space. I could've gone back and waited inside for her, I still had the key after all, but I felt wrong even thinking about doing that. I was a little guilty about not giving it back to her when she asked, but to me that felt like I was admitting defeat and that our relationship was officially over.

I knew how it must have looked to her. Some random, crazy bitch just starts yelling that I'm cheating on her in the middle of the grocery store, and of course Savannah thinks that's the truth. Of course, it was a little more complicated than just some random girl yelling, but I would never be involved with two different women at one time.

I had gone out with Brittany over six months ago. We had gone on two dates, we had slept together once, and then I had realized how clingy and needy she was. I ended things right then and there, but Brittany didn't get the message. She started stalking me. Literally. She followed me all the time, constantly getting in my path and asking why I hadn't called her.

There had been another time, where I had been on a first date with a girl, and Brittany had been following us. I hadn't known, until a similar situation had occurred. Brittany had flipped out on her and went off on me about "cheating" on her. I tried explaining to Brittany that we were never together, and I had ended things with her before they even began, months before, but she wouldn't listen to me. I eventually had to get a restraining order against her, and that seemed to ward her off for a while, but it appeared she had found me again, even if just by coincidence.

The last time it had happened, I didn't really care too much, considering that it was a first date, and I wasn't that interested in the girl to begin with, but this time, it had cost me my relationship with Savannah. I knew she was upset, but I wished she would just let me explain. I just wanted her. No one else.

"Hey, man," Phoenix said as he walked up to me at work. "Any word from Savannah?" he asked. I had told him everything that had happened, hoping he might have some insight, considering he had technically known Savannah longer than I had.

"No. She's completely stonewalling me. I need to make her listen, I just don't know how. She won't let me have any contact with her at all," I said, frustration evident in my tone.

"Well, it's obvious, isn't it? Savannah is as stubborn as a mule. You need to get in her face to explain it. She probably hasn't even read or listened to any of the messages you've left her. That's why she hasn't responded to you."

I contemplated that for a moment, and saw that he was totally right. My Savannah wouldn't ignore me if she knew the truth, and considering I had told her in multiple different messages, it had to have been that she didn't know yet.

"Dude, you're right. Jesus. I've been so upset that I haven't been able to think straight. I need to go over there tonight and make her listen to me."

"Damn straight. Took you long enough, you dumb motherfucker, you should've done this right after it happened and your sorry ass wouldn't have been moping around here for a month," Nix said in his surly, gruff way. I laughed, punching him in his shoulder, no doubt doing no damage considering how huge he was.

"Thanks, man. I needed someone to kick me in the ass."

"Anytime, asshole," Nix said, punching me back.

I finally had a plan. It was decided, I was going to go to her apartment and make her listen to me and then we would have makeup sex. All. Night. Long.

I just had to work first.

Chapter 22

Savannah

It had been a month since the grocery store incident. I was coping. I was fine, I kept telling myself. After work, I'd been drowning myself in wine and chocolate, while also watching lots of *Grey's Anatomy* and listening to endless sorrowful music to feed my depression, like Tegan and Sara and Lana Del Rey. I was also listening to Emarosa a lot, but that made me cry more than anything because it was the band that reminded me most of Charlie.

I had gone out with the girls once, and I'd hated it the whole time. We had gone out to a club (Anna's insistence), and I almost had an anxiety attack from being in such a close vicinity to so many strangers. I also had that same feeling again that someone was watching me. When it didn't disappear for the whole night, I chalked it up to me being uncomfortable around a bunch of people.

I also hadn't washed my sheets. I knew it was disgusting, but I couldn't do it. It was like erasing the last piece of him from my apartment. Sometimes, I would lie on his side of the bed and convince myself that I could still smell him.

I was going to go home after work and do the same thing I had done every night since we broke up, with the exception of that one outing. But it ended up being a very different evening than I ever could have imagined.

I came home after work, fed Jorge, poured a huge glass of wine, and camped out on the couch after I changed into the silk nightie that Charlie had gotten me. It was so comfortable, and it made me feel sexier than the huge mess that I was.

After about a half a bottle of wine, and two episodes of *Grey's Anatomy*, I heard a knock at the door. I no longer worried about it being or hoped it was Charlie. It had been a month. I knew he wasn't going to stop by anytime. I knew he had to be back with his "Brittany," and that he had forgotten all about me.

I opened the door, expecting to see one of the girls, figuring they were checking on my depressed ass. Instead, I saw someone completely unwelcome and unexpected.

"Savannah, baby, you dressed up for me, did you?" Greg said, leaning against the door frame.

"Greg? What are you doing here?" I asked, confused and on edge.

"Aren't you going to invite me in?" he asked, leaning in close to me. I immediately smelled liquor on his breath.

"Not tonight. Why don't you come back when you're sober and we can talk?" I asked, trying to placate him since he was hammered.

"I don't think so, sweetheart. I've been waiting for this and I ain't waitin' anymore."

"Well, I'm not letting you in," I said firmly.

"Oh, yes you are," he leered, leaning in to touch me.

I batted his hand away from me before replying, "No I'm not. Now get the fuck out of here!" I yelled, gearing up to slam the door in his face.

Before it closed though, he pushed it open faster than my tipsy reflexes could catch. He barged into the apartment and made quick work of shutting the door and locking it.

"Leave, Greg. I don't know how you found me, and frankly I don't care. Just get the *fuck* out of my apartment."

"Oh, darlin', you think you can get rid of me that easy? I've been waiting a long time for this opportunity and you aren't going to spoil it for me now," he said. There was an evil gleam in his eyes, the same one he had that night he wrapped his hand around my neck, and I got a sinking feeling in my stomach. I knew this time something terrible was about to happen. I didn't show him how frightened I was, however, thinking that it might spur him on.

"What are you talking about? What do you want from me? Why are you here after all this time?" I asked. I was really regretting my decision to wear this stupid nightgown and drink all that wine. Not that I was drunk, but I wanted to be completely sober for this conversation.

"One question at a time, sweetness," he replied, moving in closer so that he could stroke my cheek with his thumb.

"Don't touch me," I sneered as I pulled my face away.

"Don't pull away from me, Savannah!" he yelled as he shoved me up against the wall, slamming a hand hard right next to my head. He pinned his body against mine so that I couldn't move. One of his hands made its way down my torso, groping my breast roughly before sliding down my side, and I cringed at the contact.

"I'll tell you why I'm here. To get revenge, you bitch."

"Revenge? What are you talking about? You're the one who cheated on me."

"Your father" was all he said, a look of pure hatred coming over his features.

"What about my father? I have nothing to do with him. I don't even see or talk to him since he was arrested!" I shrieked.

"My father used to be a successful businessman. He had a decent little chunk of money in his bank account. That was, until he met your father. He met Paul Ajax at a bar when he was having a rough day, and wouldn't you know it, good ole Paul had something to make him feel better. Heroin. Got him hooked on it, and from then on, that's all he did. That was all he spent his money on. Everything that he had saved was gone so quickly you can't even imagine. All of that was supposed to be mine. That was *my* money, *my* inheritance that he fucking spent getting high. Now here I am, broke as a joke, with my dad homeless, on the fucking streets. All because of Paul Fucking Ajax," he sneered at me.

"Greg, I'm very sorry that my father did that, but I swear to you I had nothing to do with it."

"Bullshit!" he screamed in my face, spittle spraying everywhere. It was at that moment I could truly see how unhinged he was, and I considered the possibility that he had a mental disorder. It would certainly explain a lot of his behavior.

"It's true! I had no idea what was happening until after everything came out," I said, pleading, but knowing that at this point, there was no reasoning with him.

"Even if I did believe you, I don't give a shit. We've been living like paupers while you and your family had all the money in the world, taking from everyone and not giving a fuck about anyone but yourselves. Meanwhile, you make it seem like you're all trying to 'help make the world a better place.'" It seemed he had completely forgotten about the fact that I had zero money while we were together; I hadn't taken a cent from my parents when I left. However, it was clear that whatever argument I had would fall on deaf ears. He so badly wanted to paint me as the bad guy in his head, another sign that he wasn't mentally stable.

"Why now? Why didn't you do anything to me while we were dating?" I asked, trying to stall him.

"I didn't know you were his daughter while we were dating. When I saw the news and heard your mother mention your name, I put two and two together," he said smugly, thinking that he was some genius. Although Ajax isn't a very common last name, so he should've figured it out a long time ago, honestly. "Then I had to find you. I knew that you were my ticket to revenge. I decided to watch your parents' house, figuring that you would eventually show up. Finally you did. You and that douchebag. I followed you home that night. That was after of course you both fucked in your car like the little slut you are." My face filled with shame at the thought that he had watched Charlie and me have such a personal and beautiful moment together, even if from a distance.

"Well, why did you wait until now to do anything?"

"I knew I couldn't do anything with him around. After that night I decided to go home for a little while to wait it out. I just came back last week to see if he was still coming over here," he said. "To my pleasant surprise, it seems he's done with you," he breathed into my ear and forcefully bit down on my earlobe.

"Greg, just leave! Nothing has to happen tonight and no one will know." Even knowing that pleading wouldn't get me anywhere, I still had to try one last time.

"Oh, baby, then you won't be able to see what I have planned for us," he laughed menacingly.

"What are you going to do?" I asked.

"Well," he started, grinning evilly, dragging his gaze up and down my lingerie-clad body, "I think first, I'll rip this pretty little nightie off of you and shove you to the ground. Then I think I'm going to finally fuck that tight asshole of yours, since you denied me of it so many times. After that, I haven't quite decided. I might torture you a bit at my home and send your father a tape for ransom. Or maybe I'll just kill you and deliver you on his doorstep. We will see how much you please me tonight."

I could hear his breathing accelerate; he was becoming excited by the thought of such violence, and I felt physically sick at the thought that I voluntarily let him touch me in the past. How had I not seen or acknowledged how terrible and disgusting he was?

"You motherfucker," I yelled, surprising both him and myself before kneeing him in the balls. I was suddenly so angry. At everything. The fact that he was blaming me for the shit my father had pulled was the straw that broke the camel's back. I figured, at this point, he was going to do whatever he wanted anyway. I might as well give him a fight.

"That's it, you bitch. I'm done playing nice with you," he snarled as he threw me to the floor. As he descended on top of me, I went wild, scratching, slapping, punching, anything I could do to get him off of me. He slapped me hard in the face, stunning me. I could feel the blood dripping from my lip and the taste of copper on my tongue, making me gag. He finally grabbed hold of my wrists and flipped me onto my stomach, immobilizing me.

"It just turns me on more when you fight, baby," he sneered in my ear, making me realize that I was in deep shit.

Chapter 23

Charlie

I got off work and stopped to buy Savannah some flowers. I knew lilies were her favorite, so I got the biggest bundle of them that I could find. I also got her some chocolates, because let's face it, this was Savannah, and she loved chocolate.

I got to her apartment and I saw that her car was outside, so I knew that she was home. I sat in my car for a full five minutes, psyching myself up to go upstairs. I was really worried that she still wouldn't give me the time of day. I had waited and given her space. I just hoped that she would finally be able to listen to me and hear what I was telling her. That I hadn't cheated, that I was sorry about everything, sorry about hurting her, even if it wasn't done intentionally.

I took a deep breath, found my balls, and got out of the car. As I was making my way up the stairs, I had a terrible feeling. Like the type of feeling that I get right before I'm about to go into a really bad situation at work. Or the type of feeling I had right as the car pulled up to my house as it was up in flames.

I rushed up the rest of the flight. As I got to the door nothing seemed to be wrong. I didn't smell any smoke or see any signs of forced entry.

Maybe I was just overreacting. I decided to knock first, just in case. I didn't want to barge in on her and then have her be more upset with me. I knocked twice loudly on the door. No answer.

"Savannah?" I called. "Please let me in. I want to talk." I pressed my ear against the door. I heard some muffled noises. Something wasn't right.

"Charlie!" I heard Savannah yell before it sounded like someone cut her off at the very end. That was all the incentive I needed.

I tried the handle to find it locked. Luckily, I still had my key. I made quick work of the lock and barged in. What I saw would be forever burned in my brain, just like my parents' house up in flames, only this time, I would actually be able to change the outcome.

I saw Savannah facedown on her living room floor, her sexy green nightie that I bought her ripped all the way up the back, tears streaming down her face, blood dripping from her mouth, her arms pinned together behind her back, with a man on top of her with his wretched cock poised at her back entrance. He had blood streaming down his face and one of his eyes was swelling shut. Time seemed to slow down so that I could observe all of this in the span of a millisecond. It sped back up as soon as I reacted.

I lunged at him, and we rolled around on the floor. He was too stunned to really land any decent hits at first, but once he was over the shock, he got me good in the face. This, however, ended up giving me an advantage. It spurred me on even more. Every hit that he landed made me even more angry, had me picturing him hitting Savannah, and I went wild on him. I sat on top of him, my fists pummeling into his face over and over. I could feel crunching beneath my fists, bone giving way to my relentlessness.

At first my rage was so intense, all I could focus on was the feeling of pounding him again and again, but slowly, other senses started making their way back. Vision first, but my gaze was zeroed in on his face, covered in blood, unconscious. The next sense to hit me was smell. The scent of copper sat heavily in the air, from all the blood that was covering us both, along with the distinct smell of urine. He must have pissed himself in all the excitement. Then, sound came through at last.

"Charlie." Savannah finally broke through my rage.

I stopped to look at her. She had the phone to her ear and she was looking at me with a strange mixture that I couldn't decipher. Part thankful, part fearful, and part devastated.

"Yes, I need to report a break-in. We will also need an ambulance," she stated into the phone, clearly speaking with 911.

After she hung up, I went to her.

"Savannah, baby, are you okay?" I asked, touching her cheek. As soon as I asked, she broke down sobbing. I gathered her in my arms and held her until we heard sirens. I quickly grabbed her robe for her before anyone came up, knowing she wouldn't want anyone to see her in her state of undress.

Policemen and EMTs were soon flooding her apartment, and our moment to ourselves was over. We explained the situation, and I had a hard time not beating the shit out of him again hearing Savannah recount her story to the police as they dragged Greg away in handcuffs.

"Ma'am, would you like to be examined before we leave?" one of the EMTs asked.

"No."

"Savannah, you don't want them to check you out for injuries?" I asked her, wishing she would let them.

"No. I'm fine. He didn't do any damage apart from my split lip. You got here in time," she said, tearing up again.

"Okay, ma'am, but after the shock wears off, make sure to come in if something doesn't feel right."

They left, and Savannah and I were left alone inside her apartment. Jorge came up and whined at her legs. She picked him and held him to her as she rocked back and forth, trying to comfort herself. I went up to her and wrapped my arms around her. She let me. The three of us cuddled together for an undefined amount of time, before she broke away from me.

"You should get out of here and go back to Brittany. I'm sure she's wondering where you are," she said bitterly.

"Savannah, baby, you need to stop and listen to me. I have been trying to explain to you for a month what's been going on, and you won't let me," I said, frustrated. I tried to keep my voice calm, since she had just been through a trauma, but it was difficult because I was also very angry with her for not letting me explain.

"I don't need to hear your excuses, Charlie. You're a cheater, and I'm not going to be the girl that you use for it."

"Damn it, Savannah, listen to me!" I yelled. "I didn't cheat on anyone! I went on two dates with Brittany almost a year ago, before I ended things with her. She got really crazy and started stalking me. I went on a date with another girl when she showed up and screamed about how I was cheating on her. After that I got a restraining order against her, and it kept her away, up until she saw us in the store together. I swear, Savannah, I would never ever cheat on you. But now that we have that out of the way, I guess it's time for you to know that I used to be quite a ladies' man. I kind of brought the whole Brittany scenario upon myself by using women. I never meant to, but it just sort of happened. My hours at work made it difficult to have a relationship. Or at least that's what I always told myself. The truth is that I never wanted a relationship with anyone until I met you." There. I had spilled the whole dirty story and she could do with it what she wanted.

I stood there breathing heavily, watching her face. It was like she still wanted to believe that I was the bad guy, but she also wanted everything to go back to how it was. I could see the indecision on her face, and watched her struggle with herself while she decided.

"How do I know you aren't just bullshitting me?" she asked me skeptically.

"I have the restraining order at home. I don't want to leave you right now because of what just happened, or I would go get it for you to see," I said truthfully.

"Okay, I believe you. And I'm so tired from missing you. I don't have the strength to resist you anymore," she said, tears gathering in her eyes.

"Aww, baby. I am so sorry. I never wanted to hurt you, even unintentionally," I said, taking her into my arms and holding her close while she cried. After a few minutes, when her crying slowed, I scooped her up in my arms and brought her into the bathroom.

"Want to take a bath or a shower, honey?" I asked.

"Shower, please. I just want to get Greg's smell off of me before I collapse into bed with you."

I nodded in understanding, turned the shower on, and stripped her torn nightgown off her body before throwing it in the trash, figuring she would never want to look at it again. When we were both naked, I picked her up and stepped into her shower bath. I gently set her down and started cleaning her. After washing her body, I squirted some shampoo in my hands, working up a lather and giving her a nice scalp massage. Throughout the whole process, I tried to ignore the fact that Savannah was naked in my arms, but it was very difficult. As soon as I finished rinsing the conditioner from her hair, we stepped out and I took my time drying her off, and then wrapped her hair in a towel. I quickly toweled myself off and we made our way to the bedroom. She went to her dresser and pulled out my favorite Alkaline Trio T-shirt.

"I couldn't give this one back to you. I've been wearing it this last month. And I'm not sorry," she said seriously, looking at me.

I smiled, wrapping my arms around her and kissing her head.

"I'm glad that you kept it and have been wearing it and thinking of me."

"That's why I was wearing my nightgown that you bought me tonight. I switch between them. That kind of bit me in the ass though, didn't it?" she asked.

"Shh. Let's not talk about tonight. Let's just go to bed and I will hold you all night."

"Okay," she said as she climbed into bed after putting my shirt on with nothing else.

As soon as we got into bed, I pulled her back to my front and got as close to her as our bodies would allow. Savannah drifted off within minutes, no doubt exhausted from the night's events, but I stayed awake for a while, just breathing in her scent and reveling in the feel of her body against mine. When I finally drifted off, it was the most content I had felt in over a month.

Chapter 24

Savannah

"It just turns me on more when you fight, baby," Greg said. I could feel his putrid breath on the back of my neck and my ear. Despite his words I kept struggling. I was no longer the weak little girl I used to be.

"Go fuck yourself, because no one else will, asshole," I said as I threw my head back in an attempt to headbutt him.

"You fuckin bitch!" he yelled as he grabbed my hair and yanked hard, pulling my head back as far as it would go. "You are going to regret ever being born," he snarled at me.

I woke up screaming, sweat dripping down my chest, tears streaming down my face, and my scalp aching at the memory.

"Shh, baby. It's okay. I'm here. I won't let anything happen to you," Charlie murmured in my ear over and over until I finally felt calm enough to lie back down. He immediately pulled me against him, making sure not to put any weight on me so as not to freak me out.

"Make it go away, Charlie. Make me forget," I pleaded with him. He searched my eyes for a minute before nodding.

"Okay, Savannah, whatever you need. But you are going to be on top. You need to feel in control."

159

I nodded and leaned forward to kiss him. As soon as my lips touched his, everything felt right. The entire night faded away, the month that we had been separated disappeared, and it was just the two of us.

I moaned as his tongue came out to tangle with mine and his hands traveled down to my ass. He palmed it for a moment before dragging my body on top of his. I felt him already hard beneath me, and I ground my wetness against him.

The only clothing between us was the T-shirt I put on before bed, which Charlie made quick work of removing, and soon there were no barriers. He broke the kiss to latch his hot mouth around my nipple. I bit my lip and tilted my head back as I continued to grind my slick pussy against him. Charlie groaned beneath me and I felt the vibration through my chest.

"Fuck, baby," he said against my skin, "I missed you so damn much." He broke contact and looked up at me. "I don't think you understand how much I missed you. Please don't ever leave me again. It will destroy me."

"Me too" was all I said before I reached down and impaled myself on him, never breaking eye contact.

I woke in the morning to Charlie bringing me breakfast in bed. It was my favorite breakfast, mostly because it was the breakfast that Charlie always made me. Scrambled eggs with lots of cheese, bacon, toast, and a Bloody Mary.

"Good morning, my love," he said. "How are you feeling?"

"Surprisingly great. Mostly 'cause you're here with me," I responded.

"It's funny how you can have the best and the worst night of your life all on the same day."

Several different emotions crossed his face: concern, rage, relief, and the greatest was love. Instead of responding verbally, he bent and captured my lips with his. The kiss wasn't long or sexual, but just as potent. He broke away, setting my tray on the bed before going into the kitchen to grab his own.

We ate in companionable silence, just enjoying being with each other, before Jorge jumped on the bed, meowing furiously.

"Did you forget to feed the king?" I asked after taking a big swig of my Bloody, and scratching Jorge on the head.

"No, I didn't forget. I think he's trying to trick you and get another breakfast."

"He's sure taking full advantage of having you back here."

"I don't blame him. I am his favorite, you know."

"Ha! Nice try." Jorge made my point by coming up to me, purring and scraping up against me.

"Traitor," Charlie muttered to him under his breath. "So, do you have to work today?"

"Yeah, I'm supposed to be there at noon," I said.

"Baby, I don't think that you should go in today. You just had a pretty serious trauma happen to you yesterday. I think that you need to rest."

"No, I don't. I'm fine, Charlie. Yeah, what happened with Greg was super shitty, but I'm fine. I just want to go into work and take my mind off of everything."

"Savannah, I don't think that's such a good idea. You might feel okay now, but I think that it will start to hit you more when you leave your apartment."

"Charlie. I'm going to work."

He held his hands up in surrender. "Okay, babe. Whatever you want to do."

After we finished eating, I started getting ready for my day, and Charlie kept me company in the bathroom. I turned the shower on, and started undressing, and his eyes darkened as they roamed over all of the bruises on my body. They had formed really quickly, along with a split lip that was very swollen and sore. I was surprised he didn't react to the bruises the night before, but I guessed that he either wasn't able to see them well in the darker room, or that he didn't notice because he was so preoccupied with us reuniting. Either way, he noticed them now, and I saw his hands clench and unclench at his sides, his jaw muscle straining and twitching with how hard he was clenching his teeth. I walked over to him and stroked my fingers down his cheek.

"Hey, it's over. I'm okay. You saved me," I told him gently. He visibly relaxed at my words.

"I know. I just wish I had killed the fucker. I hate that I was almost too late. And I was in a sense. He still was able to hurt you."

"Hey now, I can handle a few bruises. I've been in girl fights worse than this," I joked, trying to lighten the mood.

"Girl fights, huh?" he asked, taking the bait. "That's pretty hot."

"Oh yeah. I totally fucked her up. I straddled her, slapping her, scratching her, and pulling her hair," I whispered in his ear seductively. I chuckled when he groaned.

"Get in the shower before I make you late for work," he said, slapping my ass as he made his way out of the bathroom.

I laughed as I started getting ready for the day, wincing a few times in the shower from some sore spots. When I finished, I came into the living room to see Charlie and Jorge all cuddled up on the couch watching *The Office.*

"Are you sure you want to go to work today? Your two favorite guys are just going to be here relaxing all day," he told me, trying to tempt me into staying home. He knew I loved that show.

"Nice try, mister. I'm going, but I have a short day today, so I should be home by five."

"Okay, well, please call me if you need anything. And make sure to text me in between appointments. If you don't, then I will come there to check on you." I smiled at his protectiveness.

"I will, I promise," I swore before bending down for a kiss, and heading out the door.

I walked up to the shop, feeling slightly more on edge than normal. Fuck. Maybe Charlie had been right and I should've stayed home, I thought. Oh well, too late now. I knew before I got there that it was going to be a slow day. I had only two appointments, and they were both small pieces. They would take me only a half hour each. That was another reason I decided to come in today. I knew I could manage that.

As I walked in, I saw Anna at the front desk on her phone. Her face lit up at seeing me, before she took in my busted lip and the bruises on my neck.

"What the fuck?! What happened to you?" she exclaimed as she jumped out of her chair to make her way over to me.

"It's a long story," I sighed as her fingers gently grazed along the side of my face, a look of concern washing over hers.

"Well, your appointment won't be here for another hour, and I don't have a single person today, so you better get talkin'."

I groaned in frustration before giving in. "Fine, but come back to my station with me so I can set up."

I told her the whole story, starting with Greg, and ending with Charlie, not leaving anything out. She interjected multiple times with comments and questions. When I finished going through every detail with her, a half an hour later, she went to the first place I knew she would go.

"So, are you and Charlie back together then?"

"Yes, of course. That was the only plus to this whole situation."

"So, how good was the makeup sex?" she asked.

"Anna!" I exclaimed. I knew Anna well, but she still surprised me on a regular basis. After all of that, that's where she decided to go.

"What?! You knew I was going to ask," she said unapologetically.

"Ha. I guess I did. It was phenomenal," I said, giving her what she wanted.

"Yes! I knew it!"

I laughed at her as I made my way back up to the front of the shop. My next client was always early so I decided to wait for her. She showed up within the next ten minutes, and I finished her a half hour later. I had about another hour or so before my next client showed up. I had never met him before. He had gotten my info from one of my regular clients. I always appreciated when people recommended me; it gave me a sense of pride, and loyalty to them.

After I cleaned my station, I sat at the front talking with Anna, all low-key stuff, which I appreciated after all of the drama. Sitting there, not really doing anything, I realized how exhausted I was. I thought again that maybe Charlie was right, and that I should've stayed home today, but I was too stubborn to actually admit it out loud and leave. Plus, I was already halfway through my day, I could finish it. Maybe I would take the next day off.

Before my client showed up, I decided to take a quick trip to the bathroom. As I came out, I saw a man standing at the front desk. At first glance, from behind he looked familiar, and a sinking feeling started in my stomach. He turned his head, and I got a side view of him, exposing his profile, and I started hyperventilating. It was Greg! How was he not in jail? He was coming back for me to finish what he started. My breath was coming faster and faster, and I felt the ground grow unsteady beneath my feet. I saw Anna give me a worried look, and felt like she was calling my name through a tunnel. Right before I collapsed, my last thought was that I was making this way too easy on him.

When I came to, I was lying on the couch at the front of the shop with multiple people standing over me. Anna, who was closest, and had the most concerned look on her face, one of the other tattoo artists, and the man who made me pass out. Now that he was much closer, and was facing me head-on, I could clearly see that he was not Greg. My mind was playing tricks on me, and I felt so foolish and embarrassed.

"Babe, are you okay? What happened?" Anna asked me.

"I'm fine," I said, avoiding eye contact, when, to my utter horror, I started tearing up.

"Hey, guys, why don't you leave us alone for just a moment," Anna said, dismissing everyone, giving me a reprieve from all the staring. As soon as they walked away, I was able to take a relieved breath. "Okay, girl, spill. What the hell was that all about?"

"I saw that guy from the side, and he looked exactly like Greg. I thought for a second that he somehow got out, and came back for me," I said, tears now streaming down my cheeks.

"Oh Savannah, I'm so sorry. You shouldn't be here right now. I'm going to get Jonathon to do that guy's tattoo, and you should call Charlie to come and pick you up. Or I can call him if you want me to."

"I don't want to talk about everything again. Can you call him? I feel stupid for coming in today, when I was clearly very wrong and he was very right about it," I said.

"Of course, girl, but you do know that Charlie isn't going to rub your face in this, right?" she asked.

"Yeah, I do, but I still feel stupid, and I don't want to hear myself say it again."

She nodded in understanding, grabbed my phone, and walked away to call him. I appreciated the moment to myself; I needed to get my shit together for now. I would be able to break down as soon as I got home, in the shower, alone, but for now, I needed to pull myself together. When Anna came back, I was quite a bit better, with the promise to myself that I would have my moment later.

"He's on his way, honey. He said he'll be here in five minutes, and that he loves you."

I nodded and just sat there, waiting for him to arrive. I was so grateful that Anna had been here today. She handled everything for me. The client was already back getting his tattoo with Jonathon, and was none the wiser that anything was wrong. Anna had told them both that I had low blood sugar, and that's why I passed out. I appreciated that she didn't let on that anything was out of the ordinary. I was able to hold on to a little bit of my pride at least.

True to his word, Charlie showed up almost exactly five minutes later. As soon as he saw me, he ran over to me, grabbing me and holding me tight. The tears threatened once again as soon as he touched me, but somehow I was able to keep it together. When I pulled back, he looked over every inch of me, before visibly relaxing slightly.

"You ready to get out of here, baby?"

"Yes. Please take me home," I said.

Chapter 25

Charlie

I loaded Savannah in the car, and drove us home. I had known that something like this was going to happen. I had seen it a million times with people at work. Especially the really tough ones. They were always surprised when they couldn't function like normal after a big trauma. It was always hard to watch, but it was a hundred times worse having to watch Savannah go through it. I was very glad that Anna had been there, someone who she trusted, to help her out. If I hadn't known that she would've been there, I would not have been okay with her going in.

We pulled up to her apartment, and I helped her get out. As soon as we walked in the front door, I asked her, "What do you need, honey?"

"I just want to take a shower," she said quietly.

"Okay, baby. Do you want me to make you some tea or anything?"

"Sure. Why don't you get the kettle going and I'll have some as soon as I get out of the shower," she said, avoiding eye contact.

With that she walked off toward the bathroom. I desperately wanted to go in there with her to keep an eye on her, but I knew that she needed her alone time. She hadn't been alone at all since everything had happened, and I knew she needed to process without me hovering over her. So instead, I got her tea going.

Fifteen minutes later, she still hadn't gotten out of the shower, and I was starting to worry about her. I pressed my ear to the door and heard the shower still running, but nothing else, none of the shuffling sounds that you'd normally hear. I listened for another minute, when I heard a very quiet sob. I couldn't stand it anymore, and opened the door.

When I came in, my heart broke when I saw Savannah sitting on the floor of the tub, hugging her legs to her chest, water pouring over her and though I couldn't see her tears because of the stream, I knew they were there from the way her eyes were swollen and red. I silently stripped my clothes off, and made my way into the shower with her. I turned the water slightly warmer, before sitting on the floor with her and pulling her into my lap, bringing her head to rest on my chest. She sobbed even harder, letting herself go completely. Some time later, she finally started to quiet. I reached over to turn the water off, before picking her up in my arms and carrying her out of the shower.

"Can you stand on your own, baby? I need to dry you off."

She nodded, and let me. I led her into her room to dress her in something warm and cozy, giving her her favorite shirt of mine to wear, along with some yoga pants and her thickest looking sweater.

After I got her all settled on the couch, I put Jorge next to her, and got her favorite sick movie going—*Seven Brides for Seven Brothers*. I brought her some tea and some broth that I had made while she was in the shower. I don't know why, but warm stuff to eat and drink is always the most comforting after going through a trauma.

"Baby, you need to eat," I told her, even though she probably didn't want to. "Especially since you fainted earlier."

"I'm not hungry."

"Savannah, eat," I said firmly. I hated to do it, but she wouldn't have eaten otherwise. She glared, looking ready to yell at me. I glared right back, letting her know that I wasn't going to give in, even if she was upset. At least she had gotten some of her feistiness back.

Finally she angrily grabbed the bowl of broth, and had a few spoonfuls. After the first few, she must've realized how hungry she was, because she pretty much drank the rest straight from the bowl after that. When she finished, she looked at me and smiled.

"Thanks. I didn't realize how hungry I was," she said, picking up her tea.

"Of course. Are you still hungry? I can make you something else if you want, and there's still more broth left. I could get you more and heat up some bread and butter for you?"

"Yes, that sounds perfect."

After she scarfed those down too, we settled in, and watched her favorite movie. She passed out within five minutes.

"Everything is going to be okay now, my love," I whispered to her as she slept.

Six months later...

I was so nervous, I was sweating right through my best shirt. I wanted this to be perfect, because Savannah was the perfect woman. At least, the perfect woman for me. She was at work, and I had turned our apartment into a combination between a flower shop, and a fire hazard with all of the candles I had burning. Luckily, I was a fireman, so I was prepared for anything.

I had conspired with Anna and Lauren to help me, from picking the ring out and figuring out her ring size, to helping plan the proposal and keeping me notified of when she was heading home, and making sure to take Savannah to get a manicure so that her nails would look perfect (apparently, that was an extremely important detail). They had been incredibly helpful, and I think we came up with something perfect.

Anna was at work with Savannah, and she was going to text me the minute she left the shop, and Lauren had helped me set the apartment up. Frank Sinatra was singing in the background, and I had the whole place covered in her favorite flowers, lilies and peonies, then I had a pathway of candles leading from the front door into the bedroom where I was waiting for her. Her whole room was covered in candles, and I was right in the middle of all of them. In my best outfit, sweat and all. My phone dinged with a text, and I almost jumped out of my skin.

She just left. GOOD LUCK!

I instantly became more nervous. We had been through so much in the last year, I hoped that this was the right time to do this. If I had my way, I would've married her the week we started dating.

I heard the door open, and I got down on one knee, waiting for her to come to me. I heard her gasp of breath, before the sound of her feet padding down the walkway toward me. A moment later, she entered the bedroom, the candlelight making her look like the queen she was. There were tears in her eyes as she looked down at me.

"Savannah," I started, my nerves gone upon seeing her, "from the moment we met, I felt this pull toward you, one that I had never felt before. I knew on our first date that I wanted to spend the rest of my life with you, I just had to convince you of it first.

"I have never met anyone else like you before. You're driven, and stubborn, but you're also so full of love for those you feel deserve it. I know that you would do anything for me, just as I would for you.

From the very beginning, I felt like I needed to save you, from your sadness and your past, but you were actually the one to save me. I was drowning before I found you, and you were the one to pull me out. I love you more than words could ever express. Will you marry me?"

I reached into my pocket to pull out the box. When I opened it, her eyes, which were now streaming tears into her enormous smile, shifted down to see what I had bought her. It was an antique-looking ring, rose gold, with a round-cut blue sapphire with a diamond halo and two diamonds on either side.

She looked back into my eyes and said, "Yes! Yes, of course I will!" I stood and pulled her to me, bringing my lips to hers. She was smiling against my lips and laughing the happiest laugh I had ever heard come from her beautiful mouth. We broke the kiss, and she held her left hand out for me to slide my ring on her finger. As soon as it was on, my heart soared and I kissed her finger right above the ring.

"Make love to me, future husband," she said.

"Yes, future wife."

I kissed her again, deeply, taking her clothes off as I did. She moaned into my mouth, her hands reaching for my clothes as well. When we were both completely undressed, I picked her up and set her gently in the middle of the bed. I lay on top of her, my hands roaming over her body slowly. When she was a moaning, incoherent mess, I broke away, and dragged my lips down her body until I reached her drenched, glorious cunt.

"Fuck, baby. You are soaked for me," I groaned while I swiped my finger through her folds, making her cry out.

I licked her slowly, from her entrance up to her tight bundle of nerves, and back down. I did that a few more times, making sure to tease her a bit, before I latched my mouth around her clit and sucked hard, making her squirm. She was close already, and I had barely touched her.

I alternated between sucking and licking, my mouth worshiping her, before I brought my fingers into the mix, teasing her opening. She was so wet that my fingers were instantly coated with her essence. I slowly pushed two fingers into her, switching between pumping them in and out, and moving them in a come-hither motion.

"Charlie, I'm close," she panted above me.

I doubled my efforts, pumping my fingers into her fast and deep, and when I felt her starting to clamp down on my hand, I gently bit down on her clit and she detonated, gripping my hair and gyrating hard into my face. I groaned loudly at the feel and taste of her.

When she had come down, I crawled up her body and slid into her, locking my eyes with hers. Her pussy was still spasming from her orgasm and I fought the need to come already. I withdrew, pulling almost all the way out before slowly pushing back in. I made love to her unhurriedly, wanting this to last as long as it could.

"Charlie, more please," she begged me.

"Not yet, my love. I want this to last."

I ground into her a few more times at my leisurely pace, but she wasn't having it. She wrapped her legs around my hips and pushed her heels into my ass, forcing me fast and deep into her. We both groaned loudly, my self-control snapped, and I needed no further encouragement from her. I set a frantic pace for us after that, bringing myself much too close to exploding for comfort. I needed her to come again before that could happen.

"Play with yourself, Savannah. I need you to come."

She reached down to touch herself as I took one of her nipples in between my fingertips. I kissed her deeply and twisted the tight bud hard, and a moment later I felt her pussy clamping down on my cock before she wailed into my mouth. Her orgasm set mine off, and I exploded into her a second later, staring into the eyes of the love of my life.

Chapter 26

Savannah

It had been two days since Charlie and I got engaged, and I was still so unbelievably happy that I hadn't come down from the clouds yet. Charlie had also officially moved in like two seconds later. We had always liked my place better than his, so he put his notice in for his apartment, and had slowly started moving stuff over to mine. Charlie and I had the day off together, so we decided to have a dinner party with our closest friends to share the news with them.

I started expanding my cooking abilities, and decided to make three-cheese-stuffed shells. It was relatively easy, and delicious. I also made some garlic bread and a Caesar salad to go with it, because let's be honest, what was Italian food without bread and salad? Oh, and wine, which I was drinking as I cooked.

At seven sharp, Lauren showed up with Ryan, bearing homemade tiramisu.

"Hey, lady!" she exclaimed as Charlie and I opened the door. "This is Ryan. It's about time the two of you actually met, considering how close we've become."

I hugged Lauren before shaking Ryan's hand and introducing him to

Charlie. Right after they showed up, Anna walked in, with Charlie's good friend Phoenix right on her heels. We had been hanging out with him quite a bit the last few months. I had also tattooed Phoenix in the past, and he was just as gorgeous now as he was then. He had asked me on a date that first session, but I turned him down, since it had been right after Greg and I broke up. He was tall, taller than Charlie, and more muscular too. He had naturally red hair that was short on the sides and longer on top. Usually he didn't really bother styling it, letting it just do kind of whatever it wanted, his natural waves flopping every which way, but tonight he had it in a pompadour-type style, which looked really good on him. He had hazel eyes, which I noticed switched between green and brown depending on his mood, and his facial features were fairly severe. His jaw bone was sharp and he had a very defined nose. Needless to say, very handsome.

"Hey, Phoenix, long time no see," I said jokingly since I had just seen him the week prior, leaning in to give him a hug.

"Babe, I told you, call me Nix, only my mother calls me Phoenix."

"Fucker," Charlie said, playfully punching him in the arm. "Don't call my girl pet names."

I made introductions, skipping Anna. She had pierced Nix multiple times, although the only visible piercing was his eyebrow. Anna told me about all his others, including a Prince Albert. I had often wondered if the two of them would ever get together, considering they were both single and attractive, but she assured me that it had never been that way with the two of them. The way he talked and his mannerisms reminded her of one of her exes who she had a bad experience with, which was unfortunate, she said, because he was, and I quote, "hung like a horse."

When I introduced Nix to Lauren, his eyes raked over every inch of her, before settling on the engagement ring on her left hand. His expression, which was previously heated, shut down immediately as he stepped back after shaking her hand and Ryan's. Lauren and Ryan didn't seem to notice, however, politely chatting with Nix and asking him questions. In typical Nix fashion, he didn't say much, mostly grunting in response to a lot of their questions. Then, Anna jumped in to break the ice, in her typical way.

"Nix, darling," she purred, sidling up next to him, "I haven't seen you down there in a while, does the carpet still match the drapes? Or did you finally shave that shit off?"

I choked on my wine as Nix glared at her, and I slapped Anna on the hand. "Anna! Jesus. On that lovely note, let's all eat," I said, trying to defuse the building tension. Once we were all settled and eating, small talk started again, this time it was more natural. I guess maybe Anna's strategy worked.

"So Phoenix, what do you do for work?" Lauren asked, seeming to forget that he liked to be called Nix.

"I work with Charlie at the fire station. I actually trained this dumb shit over here. Good thing too, otherwise he would be dead by now," he said, smirking at Charlie.

"Yeah, good thing, 'cause otherwise you would be dead too, considering I saved your ass last year," Charlie teased him back.

"*Sam Heughan!*" Anna shouted all of a sudden. When we all looked at her confused, she clarified. "Sorry, I just realized that's who Nix reminds me of. You know, Jamie Fraser from *Outlander?*"

"Oh no," Ryan said, "You shouldn't have told Lauren that. I'm in trouble now because that's her main celebrity crush." He winked, teasing her. She blushed, avoiding eye contact with Nix.

"Oh, you know I only have eyes for you, future husband," she said sweetly, kissing him on the cheek. Her hand then drifted to her stomach. I seemed to be the only one who noticed and decided to test my theory.

"Lauren, you didn't seem to get any wine. Do you want me to pour you some?" I asked innocently.

"Oh, umm, actually," she stammered, looking at Ryan, when he smiled at her, she turned to the group and announced, "We're pregnant!" There were exclamations around the table from all of us.

"How far along are you?" I asked.

"We just found out last week, and I just crossed the two-month mark," she replied, beaming.

"So are you guys getting married before the baby, or are you going to wait until after?" Anna asked.

"We haven't decided yet. This little one wasn't planned, so we are just trying to take our time and figure out what we want to do first," Ryan said.

"So on that subject, we actually have some news too. Charlie and I are getting married!" I announced, showing off my ring to the table.

"Dude, congrats, brother!" Nix said, smiling and slapping Charlie on the back in that manly way.

"It's about time you told us, bitch!" Anna yelled.

"Yeah! We've known for like two full days!" Lauren added.

"What? How did you guys know?" I asked, confused.

"As amazing as your fiancé is, do you really think he could have planned that phenomenal proposal without help from a woman? I mean come on, he is a man," Anna stated, laughing.

"Hey now!" Charlie exclaimed. "I did pretty damn good. I picked out the ring all by myself, and most of the proposal was my idea."

"That's true, Anna. Stop trying to take credit for all of it. Your only great idea was to have the trail of candles leading to the bedroom, and you followed it up with telling him he should be lying naked on the bed," Lauren said.

"Hey! That would've been a good idea!" I said, picturing it in my head and giving Charlie an appreciative glance.

"See! I told you guys!" Anna yelled once again. We spent the rest of the night talking, laughing and drinking, happy as could be.

A week later, Charlie and I were both working. We were having a slow day at the shop, so naturally, Anna and I were hanging out on the couch, talking.

"So have you guys set a date yet?" she asked.

"Not officially, but we're thinking about next winter, so like a year and a half?"

"Ooh, I love winter weddings! They're so classy and beautiful, and not to mention, way cheaper."

"Yes exactly! Plus that gives me plenty of time to plan, and by that time, Lauren won't be pregnant anymore, so you both can be my maids of honor."

"That was a terrible way of asking me to be your maid of honor," Anna said sarcastically.

"Oh, fine. I will send you a formal proposal. Better?" I asked, rolling my eyes.

"Absolutely. Now, once I get it, I will formally give you my reply." We both laughed, knowing that neither of us would do any such thing.

An hour later, our clients finally walked in the door, and both of us got to work. My client had been coming to me for many years, and we always had a lot of fun when she was on my table. One of my coworkers was playing Snoop Dogg, and as a result, all of us were loudly and terribly rapping, and laughing our asses off, I might add.

I had just finished up cashing out my client, when my cell rang. *Charlie.*

That was weird. He was still at work, and he rarely ever called me while he was working.

"Hey, babe. What's up?" I answered. There was a lot of noise in the background.

"Savannah, baby. Something has happened."

I got a sinking feeling in the pit of my stomach.

"What? What is it?" I asked frantically. Anna, hearing my tone, came over to see if everything was okay.

"Honey, you need to come to Denver Health hospital. As soon as you can."

"Oh my God. Why? Who is it?"

"It's Lauren. Lauren was in an accident."

Author Notes

Want more? Read Lauren's story next. *Light Me Up* is coming soon!
Sign up for my newsletter to get all the latest on my new books!
http://eepurl.com/hRZzz5

Thank you all so much for reading! I had so much fun writing this story, and I hope you had just as much fun reading it.

This is the first novel I've ever written, and it's started me on such an exciting path! I really hope you keep reading and stick with me on this journey.

If you enjoyed this book, please leave a review for me. Thank you so much!

I love hearing from my readers! Find me on...
Instagram–L.J.Burkhart.author
Pinterest–Ljburkhartbooks
Email–LJBurkhartbooks@gmail.com
Website—https://ljburkhart.wixsite.com/ljburkhartbooks

Acknowledgments

I would like to thank lots of people for helping me in this long, overwhelming, and exciting journey.

First of all, my husband. You have been there with me through this whole process since the very beginning. Without your love, support, and belief in me, I never would have gotten this far.

To all of my friends and family, who have proofread and helped edit this entire book. It was all of your excitement and wonder of what was to come next that inspired me to keep going.

To my mother, thank you for always believing in me. You also gave me your incredible writing talent and your appreciation for men, both of which have contributed a great deal to this story.

To my editor, Beth, I appreciate all of your hard work on this project with me, not to mention your understanding and patience, explaining everything to me on my first novel. You've been fantastic and I'm excited to continue working with you!

To my graphic designer, Les, thank you for bringing my vision to life in my cover. You present beautiful work, and I'm so lucky to have found you.

Lastly, to my readers. I am very excited to be able to share this with you. You all motivated me to keep going so I was able to give this to you. I couldn't have done it without the promise of you.

About the Author

L.J. Burkhart is the author of the new novel *Fire & Ink*. She writes contemporary romance and may eventually venture into fantasy. Her latest works are the sequels in the *Fire & Ink* trilogy, *Light Me Up* and *The Fire Inside Me*. L.J. has been a lifelong writer, starting with songs and poetry in the third grade, before eventually moving on to novels in her early twenties. When she isn't coming up with dramatic plot twists and steamy sex scenes, you can find her doing yoga, hanging out with her best bitches, baking, or reading, curled up on the couch with her husband and dog with a big glass of red wine.

You can connect with me on:

- https://ljburkhart.wixsite.com/ljburkhartbooks
- https://www.instagram.com/l.j.burkhart.author
- https://www.pinterest.com/ljburkhartbooks

Subscribe to my newsletter:

- http://eepurl.com/hRZzz5

Made in the USA
Middletown, DE
06 November 2023

41955247R00111